Bidding on
the Billionaire

Bidding on the Billionaire

JM STEWART

FOREVER
YOURS

New York   Boston

Forever Yours
Hachette Book Group
1290 Avenue of the Americas
New York, NY 10104
hachettebookgroup.com
twitter.com/foreverromance

First ebook and print on demand edition: March 2016

Forever Yours is an imprint of Grand Central Publishing.
The Forever Yours name and logo are trademarks of Hachette Book Group, Inc.

The publisher is not responsible for websites (or their content) that are not owned by the publisher.

The Hachette Speakers Bureau provides a wide range of authors for speaking events. To find out more, go to www.hachettespeakersbureau.com or call (866) 376-6591.

ISBN 978-1-4555-9218-0

This one goes to my long-time critique partner, Skye Jones. This series wouldn't even be here if you hadn't encouraged me to try. A thousand thank-yous.

Bidding on
the Billionaire

Chapter One

The musical ding of an incoming chat sounded through her laptop's speakers. Hannah Miller's heart stuttered. Standing in her kitchen, coffee cup in hand, electricity fizzled along her nerve endings, settling hot and luscious between her thighs. She didn't need to see them to know what they said. The same words popped up every night: *Hey baby. You there?*

Like every night, the same little flutter of excitement and arousal slid through her. Every inch of her came alive. He was early tonight. According to the clock on her cable box, it was ten past seven. They didn't usually meet until sometime around nine. She'd anticipated a couple of hours of waiting.

She bit her lower lip, gnashing it between her teeth. What she needed to do was wait before answering him. Keep him wondering. She didn't want to look too eager. Like she hadn't been biding her time waiting…in lingerie she'd bought just for him.

She glanced down at herself, fingering the hem of the pink negligee she'd donned an hour before. The sheer fabric fluttered over the tops of her thighs. It was the first time she'd ever splurged for something sexy, but on the way home from the bookshop this afternoon, she got to thinking about him and ended up in the Victoria's Secret on Pine Street. It was a spur-of-the-moment splurge. She'd taken one look at it and knew he'd love it.

She had to admit, wearing the see-through nightie filled her with a sense of feminine power. She *felt* sexy. Something she hadn't felt since long before her breakup with Dane a year and a half ago.

She sighed, set her cup on the counter, and gave in to the pull. Then she moved around the breakfast bar separating the kitchen from the living room and padded across the space. As she came to stand behind the couch, she rested her hands along the back and stared at the words on the screen. It had to be pathetic to look forward to a date with a man she'd never met. Night after night, she sat alone in front of her computer. The only sexual gratification she'd gotten in the last year and a half always happened solo.

She didn't even know the guy's real name. She'd been chatting with him for six months now. They'd met on a message board discussing a book, an erotic romance of all things. An easy friendship had developed that had become more over time. He made her laugh. He challenged her. And he made her see stars. She knew intimate things about this man. Where he liked to be touched and how, what his kinks were, his hopes and dreams.

Yet all she knew about *him* was that he was Harley-riding lawyer from San Diego. They chatted via Gchat and both went by anonymous usernames. She was "JustAGurl456." He didn't offer his real name, and she didn't ask. He could be her neighbor for all she knew, the ugly guy in 45B who played the weird music at two in the morning.

Still, she looked forward to this part of her day, to coming home knowing he'd be there. Even if all they did was chat about their days, he was a lure she could never resist. More often than not, though, their conversations veered toward the hot and erotic. The man had magic fingers. He always knew the right thing to say to light her on fire, and those fingers always reached through the wires straight into her core.

She'd throbbed all day thinking about her chat with him. So much so she'd stopped on the way home for something sexy to describe to him. She only wished her lover could be there to see the nightie she'd bought for him. She'd even contemplated getting brave and sending him a picture or inviting him to a video chat on Skype. She'd grown tired of her own fingers. Even her high-end vibrator didn't cut it anymore. What she craved was touch and the warmth of skin. A flesh-and-blood lover.

Except she'd never been able to summon the courage to move beyond their anonymous chats. She had rules she'd lived by since her parents' deaths, since she ended up in a children's home and part of the foster care system. Inserted and forgotten. She'd set those rules aside for Dane. Since his exit from her life, she'd reaffirmed them. The top one? Never get attached. She was already growing attached to this one. The fact that she was here, waiting, proved it. She knew better.

Even knowing that, she moved around the couch and sat, picked up her laptop, and set it on her knees. As she punched in a reply, her hands trembled with nerves and the first stirrings of arousal. Yeah. This was why she was so damn addicted to him. Because all he had to do was pop up in her Gchat window and her panties dampened.

JustAGurl456: Hi. You're home early tonight. I didn't expect to see you until after nine.

bikerboy357: Meeting canceled last minute. Paperwork can wait. I had to talk to you. I've been looking forward to you all day.

JustAGurl456: Mmm. Me too.

Hannah inserted a finger into her mouth, biting down on the nonexistent nail. She shouldn't have told him that. Did she sound too desperate?

bikerboy357: Did you have a good day?

JustAGurl456: I had a long day. You?

Her day had been slow and boring. A couple of requests from her online bookstore had come in, people looking for original first copies, but the shop itself had been slow. Being in the middle of the rainy season for Seattle, the day had been dreary, the light drizzle enough to keep people indoors. Despite the shop sitting around the corner from Pike Place Market, only a handful of customers had come into the physical store.

bikerboy357: I've had a helluva hard-on all day thinking about you. Made the day hella long. Let's do something crazy tonight, baby.

That he'd been looking forward to her, too, had her insides clenching in anticipation. The mention of his cock had fantasies filling her mind, and the desire to see him flared to life in her chest. It wasn't the first time the urge had hit. She had a million fantasies about what he looked like. It was her favorite. She always imagined he had big hands and a big cock. More than a time or two she'd wanted to ask him to take a picture of it. She ached to have him in front of her, to see the bulge in his slacks. She bet he was long and thick, with a bulbous head she'd kill to wrap her lips around.

Really, what she wanted, what she craved more than chocolate…was his touch. To have him beside her. To bring their online encounters into reality. She yearned for the hands touching her to be his. To open her eyes after an intense, mind-blowing orgasm and find herself alone always filled her with emptiness. She was tired of being alone.

JustAGurl456: OK. What do you have in mind?

bikerboy357: Let me call you. I know we agreed to keep this anonymous, but I'm dying to hear your voice.

Her scintillating mood skidded to a halt. For a moment, all she could do was blink at the screen. Call her? Was he serious? Her hands trembled again, this time from the nerves currently wrapping themselves around her throat. Okay, she'd admit it. She'd fantasized about talking to him on the phone, actually getting to hear his voice. It would make him seem a little closer, a little more human and not just words on a computer screen.

She'd told this man secrets she'd never told anyone, including her best friend, Maddie. Like how lonely she really was. It was something they shared. A love for reading…and a lonely emptiness nothing could fill. There were nights when they simply chatted, about life and horrible days and wishes and dreams. He'd become a friend, and she looked forward to their chats as much as she did nights like these when she craved his body the most.

She'd made her self-imposed rules to protect her heart. If one more person left her life, she might crawl up inside herself and never come out. Those rules, however, isolated her. The loneliness and monotony of her life got to her every once in a while. She longed to hear his voice, to hear the sounds he made when his orgasm ripped through him. Even to know the sound of his laugh.

Letting him call her, though, would take their exchanges to a level she didn't know if she was ready for. What did she know about this guy, really? Nothing. Well, okay, almost nothing. She knew his favorite color was blue, that he had a love for good Chinese, and that he was a reader, like her, but she couldn't pick him out of a lineup. She had no idea if he had siblings, or if he even had family at all. He was little more than a chat handle on the other side of her computer. One step above a fantasy. How did she know he hadn't lied about himself, the way she had?

Truth was, as lonely as it could get, she preferred their relationship this way. At least online, he wouldn't be able to see her. He wouldn't discover she'd lied about her looks. She didn't have long legs up to her ears or blond hair. She had mousy brown locks that frizzed when it got too hot and a short, plump stature. Maddie, her business partner and best friend, insisted on calling her *curvy*. But Hannah knew she had twenty pounds she couldn't lose for the life of her and that men tended to overlook her.

She also wouldn't have to watch the disgust wash across his expression when his gaze landed on the hideous scars cutting across her face. She wouldn't have to watch him stumble for an excuse, a reason why he needed to back out of an encounter with her. She'd heard the excuses one too many times. Maybe from jerks, but still. She didn't have it in her to start all over again.

Another message popped onto her screen.

bikerboy357: Hey, where'd you go?

With shaking fingers, she punched in a quick reply.

JustAGurl456: Sorry, I'm here. I have to admit, you caught me by surprise.

bikerboy357: I want to hear your voice, baby. I want to hear your breathing when you're pumping those fingers into yourself and what sounds you make when you come all over them. I want to know you're right there with me.

A hot little shudder ran the length of her spine, settling warm and luscious in all those places he mentioned. Her clit throbbed, begging her to take him up on his offer. She'd done safe for so long it had become habit, because the fear of history repeating itself froze her into inaction. Could she do this, though?

bikerboy357: Are you nervous?

She bit her lower lip, staring at his words on the screen. The answer came immediately. She shouldn't tell him, though. No, what she ought to do was stick to the script. So far she'd played fearless and flirty, everything she wasn't in real life. She enjoyed her online persona. For a while, she could be someone more exciting, instead of the book geek who hid in the shadows.

In real life, she owned a bookstore with her best friend, Madison O'Riley. They sold rare, hard-to-find books. Hannah was a geek. She'd survived her time growing up by sticking her nose in a book, by learning to keep her eyes open while blending in with her surroundings.

Truth was, she was scared of her shadow most of the time. When she became comfortable with someone, she could talk their ear off, but in real life, she was a wallflower. Online, she was safe, because nobody could see her. They couldn't reject her before they'd even gotten to know her, and she didn't have to worry about people leaving her life. If she admitted he terrified her, she might as well admit she'd lied about her persona, too, which would do nothing but change the entire dynamic of their relationship.

The word typed itself onto the screen anyway. She had to be honest or come up with a flimsy excuse, and she hated lying, especially to him. She might not be able to pick him from a lineup, but she knew one thing—he really was a nice guy, lonely like her, and lying to him made her feel too much like the very thing she loathed.

JustAGurl456: yes

Seconds passed. She bit down on her nail again, nervousness clutching at her stomach. Had she scared him off by being too honest?

bikerboy357: 312-555-1725. That's my cell number. How 'bout you call me then.

Her gaze shot to her phone, lying on the coffee table across from her. Its dark shape beckoned, daring her to pick it up. She swallowed hard. The thought of talking to him had become her latest fantasy. Getting to hear the sexy sound of his voice and the noises he made when he came. His breath sawing in and out as his arousal ramped up, as they pushed each other to the point of no return and he tipped over the edge with her. Yeah, she wanted that. Desperately.

Another message popped onto her screen.

bikerboy357: All right, honesty time? I'm dying to know the sound of your voice. It would make you feel not quite so far away. I hate that I can't see you or touch you. You're a big

part of my day, but I don't even know what your laugh sounds like.

His admission tugged at the isolated place inside. She couldn't deny she yearned for the same things. Or that she'd had the very same thoughts.

Then and there the decision made itself, and she snatched her phone off the table. It didn't have to change things. He still wouldn't be able to see her.

Her fingers trembled as she punched in his number, and she hesitated at the last digit, her thumb hovering over the CALL button. She couldn't go back after this.

bikerboy357: I always imagined you'd have a sweet voice. I can close my eyes and pretend you're here with me.

Oh God, that did it. It was like he'd snatched the thought right out of her head. Knowing he understood what it was to be lonely made talking to him irresistible. She swallowed down the fear and punched the CALL button before she lost the nerve. As the phone rang, her heart rate skyrocketed, a dull pulsing in her ears. She squeezed her eyes shut and took a deep breath in a desperate attempt not to sound as nervous as she felt. With any luck, her tongue wouldn't trip over itself.

Please, God, don't let me say something stupid.

The line rang once, then twice. Her breath stalled as she waited for the click, for a voice to sound on the other end of the line. Was he as nervous as she was?

"Hey."

His voice rumbled along the line, low and etched with a happy edge. Hot little shivers raced along the surface of her skin and a stupid smile stretched across her face. She'd thought of this moment a million times, and he fulfilled the fantasy. He had a sexy bedroom voice, deep and powerful but quiet, one she could envision listening to while lying in the dark. The thought of the naughty things he'd whisper in her ear had fire licking along every nerve ending.

She settled back on the couch and closed her eyes. "So why not find a real woman?"

"You're not real?"

His voice held an amused tease, and her pulse skipped. He had a sense of humor. A man with a sense of humor was sexy as hell.

"I'm a voice on the other end of the phone."

Another silence. This one longer.

"Actually, I consider you a friend. Someone I'd like to meet in real life. I've been thinking about that a lot lately. But to answer your question, it's…complicated."

The uneasy edge in his voice had her opening her eyes. She sat up, her heart skipping a panicky beat. "Complicated? You don't have a wife, do you? Be honest."

He laughed. The deep, sexy rumble had hot little waves rolling through her belly. "No. No wife, I promise. Just too much life. What's your name, sweetheart?"

Oh God. He had to ask her that. They'd agreed on this early on. For the sake of anonymity, she hadn't wanted to know his real name. That had to be pathetic. She had a lover whose name she didn't know and whose face she wouldn't recognize on the street if she passed him.

She drew a shaky breath and released it. She could do this. Hadn't she always wanted to move beyond her fear of being judged? She hadn't had a real date in over a year. The last one ended in disaster. The guy, a man she met on a match-matching website no less, had taken one look at her face and made excuses, like all the others.

She hadn't had sex for even longer, when her college sweetheart announced, out of the clear blue sky, that he'd fallen for someone else. She and Dane had met her first year in college. He was her first love, her first everything. She'd lost her virginity to him. They'd spent five years together, all through college and a year beyond. He dumped her a year ago when he announced he was getting married. Had cruelly pointed out his new fiancée was someone less encumbered and more exciting. He'd called her vanilla.

"I'd like a name to put to the voice. Truth is, as addicted as I am to our chats, I miss the human element. I've been dying to make you a little more real."

The hunger in his tone made her throb. She couldn't *not* answer him. This might be a fantasy, but it kept her going. She needed this. "H-Hannah. My name is Hannah."

He let out a quiet, thoughtful little "hmm." "That's a very sexy name. It's nice to meet you, Hannah. I'm Cade. Tell me about you, baby. What do you do? You never told me. You're always shrouded in mystery."

She settled deeper into the couch, letting the image of him wash over her and the husky timbre of his voice settle her nerves. "I don't want to talk. I want you to make me come. Tell me what you're wearing."

She didn't want to get to know him or consider him as anything more than what he was—some random guy whose hot voice and sexy words made her come so hard he often left her gasping for breath. Something she never achieved alone. Yes, she wanted more, but to give in to the urge was dangerous at best.

Cade tsked, low and amused. "You're always all business. Do you ever relax?"

"That's what you are. You're my vacation from life. Except I can't see you, so you're going to have to fill in the blanks for me."

"That can be arranged, you know. Us meeting, I mean. Tell me you haven't thought about it."

Her heart stalled. She touched the scar running down the side of her face. She had thought about it, a lot, but just the mention of meeting him in person had panic clawing its way through her chest and closing its icy hands around her throat. Envisioning his reaction, the disgust in his eyes when he looked at her...

She squeezed her eyes shut, her breathing coming harsh and shallow. He was ruining the moment, ruining her high by bringing reality into their exchange. He'd changed the rules, damn it.

She opened her eyes, desperate to drag this back to where it ought to be. "Are you hard, Cade? Is your cock in your hand yet? I bought lingerie for you today. A little see-through number. You can see my nipples. They're hard. Just for you."

He growled again, a muted sound that was half needy groan. The sound a man made when he was aroused and desperate for relief. "All right, I give. I'm hard as steel and you're the reason. And since you asked so nicely, I'm thinking about *you*. I want to know what you look like, every curve of your body. I want to be able to look into your eyes, know your smile. I yearn to know the feel of your skin. God, I bet it's so soft."

His words and the hunger within them shivered all the way down her spine, settling in a desperate place. Getting to hear him made breaking protocol worth every nervous heartbeat. She wanted to add to her fantasy, to ramp it up, so when she lay in the darkness of night, easing the ache by herself for the hundredth time, she wouldn't feel so alone. She had another aspect to make her fantasy a little more tangible. She'd never admit it to him, but she yearned for the same thing. For him to be standing in front of her. To know the warmth of his skin, the softness of his mouth, and the strength of his embrace as he closed his arms around her.

She couldn't risk it, though. They had something good here. She craved more, the physical touch of his hands on her body, but hearing his voice would have to do because she wouldn't take the chance he'd end up like all the rest. She'd broken the rules with Dane and look where it got her. "Please don't make this difficult. This isn't what we agreed on."

He sighed heavily. "I'm sorry. I know it's not, but I'm addicted to you. God, I can't even tell you. I haven't had dinner yet, haven't even taken off my tie, but I had to talk to you. You're the first thing I want as soon as I get home. I'm hard all day because I look forward to talking to you at night. And up until tonight, I didn't even know your name. I don't know what you look like either, just what you've told me, and I crave it."

She closed her eyes and drew a shuddering breath. Knowing he looked forward to their chats as much as she did relaxed a knot in her stomach. Somehow, right then, it made him more than just a figment of her vivid imagination. She wanted to ask him, again, why he didn't find a flesh-and-blood woman, a one-night stand, but he continued before the words could leave her tongue.

"I'm going to be in Seattle next week. In fact, most of my clients are in Seattle. It's where my family's from. I grew up there.

I go there a lot for business. The thought of being there and not getting to see you is driving me crazy. I've been back twice since we met, and every time I come, I have the same desire. To see you." He paused. "Have coffee with me. Only coffee. We can play it by ear from there. I have to see you, baby."

God, he had no idea how tempted she was. She couldn't deny she wanted the same thing. She'd thought of little else for weeks. What he looked like. The curve of his lips when he smiled and the broadness of his chest. How his hands would feel sliding over her skin.

It was long past time to distract him. "Take your cock out, Cade. Stroke it for me, long and slow."

Another moment of silence rose between them. Had she pushed too hard? Had she ruined the moment for him?

Finally he sighed, a sound of acquiescence.

"All right, baby. We'll play it your way. I'm too desperate to argue with you." The sound of a zipper being pulled down came over the line, whisper soft, and Cade released a ragged breath. "My cock's out. The sound of your voice has me so turned on. I'm stroking for you, long and slow, the way you like it. Tell me what you want me to do. I'm all yours."

Grateful for the change in subject, she closed her eyes and immersed herself in the sound of his voice, in the fantasy he represented. She slipped her hand into her panties and dipped her fingers inside herself. The sound of his voice turned her on as well. She was already wet, and her clit pulsed, sending a gratifying rush of delight when she caressed it with the tip of her thumb. "Tell me what you're thinking about while you stroke."

He let out a quiet, shuddering breath. "You. I'm wishing like hell this was your mouth wrapped around me. I'm imagining what you'd look like on your knees at my feet, looking up at me."

And just that easy, the desire flared like a glowing bonfire between them. It was the way it always was with him. So easy. They'd started out arguing opposite sides of the book they were reading. The attraction between them had grown as organically as the trees outside her apartment building. The sound of his voice had added a touch of reality and her body responded to the urgency in his.

She gasped as her mind took his hot image and ran with it. Her clit pulsed again in response to the images bombarding her thoughts. "God, I want that, too."

He grunted this time, a desperate, frustrated sound. "You're killing me, you know that? You have no idea how much I wish you were here. Slip your fingers into your pussy, baby. Be my hands. Tell me what you feel like."

She did as he asked, imagining him beside her, that her fingers were his. The sweet invasion had every sensitive nerve ending coming alive, and she gasped. "I'm so wet. You have me so turned on."

"You like hearing my voice." His held a hint of amusement.

She bit her lower lip. Her fingers stilled as her nerves rose again. Did she dare tell him the truth? Some part of her said she shouldn't, but the word left her mouth anyway. She never could resist telling him things she shouldn't. Like how much she wanted *him*. "Yes."

"Me too. You have the sexiest voice. Soft and sweet. I'm on the edge already. Have been all damn day, but your voice… God, your voice turns me on. Tell me what you'd do to me if I were there."

She swept her index finger over her clit. Her breathing ramped up a notch, coming in short rasps. Her mind filled with the images. Of him, seated on a couch, like her, his shirt open, tie crooked, pants unbuttoned. Oh yeah. She knew exactly what she'd do if she were there. "I want exactly that. I'd drop to my knees at your feet and suck your cock."

"You like that, baby?"

This time, his words came low and quiet. His voice had taken on an edge, and his breathing became a soft, erratic huff in her ear. It had her envisioning him closing his eyes, dropping his head back, losing himself in her voice as his hand stroked the length of his cock. The desperate edge in his voice made her wonder...was he as close to coming as she was? The thought only made her hotter.

She slid her fingers over her clit, circled, then down her slit and inside, working them in and out, imagining they were his instead. Every pump of her fingers tossed her closer and closer to the edge. Hearing his desire had ramped up her body's reaction. The fantasy filled her mind, of them watching each other, and had her orgasm hovering just beyond reach.

God, how was it possible to be this hot already, just from hearing his voice? "I'd love to suck you. I always imagined you were long and thick. Are you leaking? I'd lap it up with my tongue."

He drew a shuddering breath and let out a quiet curse. "God, I want you. I'm so damn close. The sound of your voice is making me crazy. I ache to be inside you. I want to fuck you until neither one of us can walk. Until you scream my name and come around me. You have me tied in knots, baby."

His words sent her over the edge. Her climax struck like a

starburst, erupting through her. Colors exploded behind her eye-lids. Muscles tightened and loosened, her heaving body clamping around her fingers as a rush of white-hot pleasure washed through her. She cried out, pumping her fingers harder in an at-tempt to make her orgasm last as long as possible.

Cade's groan echoed over the line, low and etched with the same desperation and intense satisfaction rushing through her. In a flash, the image filled her mind. His eyes squeezed shut, his fist pumping as jets of his come covered his chest and belly…

The image had another wave rushing over her, this one stronger than the last. Her body bowed off the couch. Her pussy clenched around her fingers, the intensity seeming to rip her apart at the seams.

When the wracking spasms subsided, she collapsed back into the couch, panting and spent. They sat in silence, only the sound of their combined breathing, harsh and erratic, between them. She wanted to thank him. She hadn't come that hard in…prob-ably ever. It had been years at least since she'd last felt the sweet, sleepy lull of sexual satisfaction. The words, however, wouldn't leave her mouth. Exhaustion seeped over her limbs. Her eyelids drooped, her boneless body melting into the soft cushions.

"I have to see you, Hannah. That was incredible. Jesus, I think I saw stars. Think about what it would be like for real. My cock. My fingers. My mouth. On you. All over you. God, I'm hard again just thinking about it. We can make it happen. I'm going to be in Seattle for two weeks. Tell me you don't crave the real thing the way I do."

The desperation in his voice grabbed her, jerking her from the luscious lull of satiation. She couldn't deny she wanted the same thing. Lying there with her fingers still buried inside of herself, alone on her living room couch, the emptiness of her life settled over her. The way it always did when their exchanges ended.

She opened her eyes as the inherent intimacy of what they'd shared hit her full force, gripping her chest. Truth was, she wasn't a one-night-stand kind of girl. Deep down, she wanted a full relationship, and that part of her said he ought to be there beside her. Up until this point, their online affair had kept her going and eased the ache with little risk. Over the course of the last few minutes, however, it had lost its appeal. All because he'd broken protocol and had her call him. She'd heard his voice, had come so hard she lost her breath, and she craved more. Masturbating would never be the same. It would never again be enough.

She slipped her fingers from herself and sighed. "You're right. I need the real thing. I need *you*."

"Then meet me." Another plea filled with all the same hunger that had her shaking.

"But how do I know you aren't some weirdo who's going to kidnap me or kill me?" She shouldn't have asked him that. She should have turned him down flat and removed the unbearable temptation right then and there. Talking to him had always been easy. It was what pulled her to him and made him so damn terrifying at the same time.

He laughed. "You're right. It's a risk, I know. How about we meet in public? At the base of the Space Needle. I'll wear a red tie so you'll know it's me. That way, you can see me, but I can't see you. Then you can decide if you want me, too."

She was touched he'd go through so much trouble for her but reached up to touch the scar running from her temple to the corner of her chin. The night she'd gotten it came to mind. The darkened car, the twisted metal. Her parents died that night and her life changed. She'd gotten teased so much growing up that she'd come to expect it. Kids could be shallow and cruel, even in college. It didn't help that she'd gotten good grades and preferred her own company. She was a geek, a loner. She enjoyed reading. Her love for it had been what made her decide to use the meager inheritance her parents had left to open her bookstore.

Over the years, she'd been laughed at and discussed like she didn't exist, didn't have feelings. She'd overheard one too many dates in college, before she'd met Dane, talking to friends about the hideousness of her scar. Some had even laughed at her. Granted, they were drunken college boys too full of themselves, but the hurt had stuck. Since her breakup with Dane, she'd given up dating altogether. No, trying to find someone real, who'd accept her, scars and short, "voluptuous" stature and all, wasn't worth the headache.

She still had needs, though, and desires. She was twenty-five, single, and sexually frustrated. She had yet to have a wild fling for the hell of it. She lived like an old spinster, because she was afraid to live. She wanted and craved hot, heavy sex, the kind where you couldn't keep your hands off each other. Where you made out in elevators, like in the novel that brought her and Cade together in the first place. With a man, not the boys she managed to find. One who wouldn't be horrible behind her back or even to her face, who'd make her feel sexy while he fucked her into next week.

She wasn't, however, naïve. She knew better than to meet a complete stranger without knowing anything about him. "What's your last name?"

"So you can look me up? Smart girl. McKenzie. My full name is Caden Declan McKenzie, but most people call me Cade. I work for my father. Do a search on my name. I guarantee you'll find me. Now, you have to promise you aren't going to stalk me."

The playful tease in his tone had her imagining his smile, and the knot in her chest unraveled. She couldn't help a soft laugh. "I can guarantee I won't. It's not my style, but I guess you're going to have to trust me. Providing you are who you say you are, when would you like to meet?"

He was silent a moment. "You have a fantastic laugh, you know that? My flight lands Sunday night. Monday and Tuesday I'm booked solid. By the time I get back to my hotel at night, I won't be worth anything. Wednesday afternoon is free, though."

"I can do Wednesday. About three-ish?" She could pull J.J. in a couple hours early.

She and Maddie had hired J.J. a few months ago, needing someone to close the shop at night. Her little bookshop wasn't very big, little more than a small bedroom. When she'd opened it, though, she and Maddie had a dream, to do what they loved doing. Maddie was good with people. The shop had done better than either of them expected. It had grown steadily over the last three years.

Just recently, they'd lengthened their days at the request of more than a few customers, who couldn't make it in before the store closed at six. So, they kept it open until ten now. Last week, Hannah had covered her shift so J.J. could celebrate her first anniversary. Technically, that meant J.J. owed her one, though she knew the middle-aged woman wouldn't have a problem with returning the favor. It was why they'd hired her. She shared the same passion for books, and she had a sweet, need-to-please dis-position. The customers loved her. This way, Hannah would have time to go home and decide what to wear before meeting Cade at the Space Needle.

"Three it is. See you Wednesday, Hannah."

The anticipation in his voice sent a shiver of the same trickling down her spine. "I look forward to it, Cade."

And did she. More than she probably ought to.

Chapter Two

It had to be her.

Cade McKenzie leaned against the pillar, hands shoved deep into the pockets of his slacks. He'd been there for twenty minutes now, waiting, his stomach tied in nervous knots. He tried for an air of causal aloofness, as if he'd come for the scenery and could stand there all day. Any other time, he might have enjoyed exactly that. Used to his constant supply of sun in San Diego, he hadn't looked forward to the weather so famous around these parts this time of year.

He'd grown up in Seattle, born and raised. His parents still lived in the same old house in Redmond. He'd been living in San Diego, though, since he passed the bar exam and went to work at one of the branch offices for his father's law firm. He had to admit he didn't miss the constant gray so prevalent in the Pacific Northwest. For mid-March, though, the day had turned out beautiful. Bits of blue sky peeked through the usual thick cover of gray clouds, warming what might have otherwise been another dreary Seattle day.

Standing there, waiting, his nerves had long since frayed. Hannah was late. Across the grassy expanse surrounding the base of the Space Needle, though, a small brunette stood with her arms folded. She'd been there for a good ten minutes now. It was a fluke he'd even noticed her, except she was watching him. He'd caught her stare twice now, and both times, she'd blushed to the roots of her hair. Any other time, her stare might not have bothered him, except he couldn't help wondering…was that Hannah?

He hadn't slept at all the night before. He'd done what he shouldn't have and called her again. They'd spoken every night since the first time a week ago. The sweet sound of her voice wrapped around him like soft velvet. He'd become seriously addicted to her. She had a sweet nature. She was sassy and sensual. Talking to her, getting to hear the velvet of her voice, had only ramped up his need for her. One hello lit a full-on blaze inside of him. Her, too, from the sounds she made. Her moans had gotten more emphatic with each conversation. Calling her had made their already-hot exchanges damn near combustible. Each round over the last few days had grown more and more intense.

And so it had been the night before. He'd fallen asleep to the sound of her high-pitched cry still ringing in his mind. He'd tossed and turned all night to the most torturous of dreams, waking with the hard-on to end all hard-ons. The damn thing hadn't abated all day, making the meetings he'd flown out here to attend damned inconvenient. He was supposed to be concentrating on this merger, but Hannah had taken a firm place in his mind. The thought of finally getting to see her had him riding a razor-sharp edge. He'd been walking around with his hands in his pockets all damn day, trying to hide an erection. He couldn't stop wondering what she looked like, what would cross her features when she saw him. Would it even be the same in person?

The woman across the way drove him nuts. She didn't at all match the description Hannah gave him the first night they met. He expected a tall, willowy blonde with short, pixie-cut hair and long legs. This woman had light brown locks that fell past her shoulders in thick waves. She didn't look very tall, either, but short and voluptuous. She wore a gray, off-shoulder T-shirt, with a white tank beneath. Her fitted black jeans hugged her luscious curves, and his runaway libido ramped up a notch. It couldn't possibly be her, but he had to admit, if it was, he wasn't disappointed.

People came and went, passing through the area or moving beyond him to take their place in line, to go up to the observation deck of the Space Needle. There had to be several dozen women in the vicinity, but none seemed to pay him any mind. This one watched *him* the way he watched her. But was that Hannah?

Deciding to grab the bull by the horns, he turned his head and met her gaze again. Like before, a deep pink suffused her cheeks. She looked down at the ground. Following her gaze, he noted her open-toed sandals. Shoes like that said casual and comfortable but practical, which didn't at all match the carefree spirit his Hannah had always been. As he continued to stare, her gaze wandered back to him, the way it had the last few times. She peeked at him from beneath her lashes and blushed all over again.

His cock twitched in his pants. Damn it all to hell. Hannah

hadn't been shy in the least. His Hannah would have marched over here by now.

The thought that she might have lied had his nerves scattering. Hannah flat out scared the hell out of him. The fiasco that had been his ex-fiancée, Amelia, should have kept Hannah in the safe territory of the Internet. He'd discovered too little too late that Amelia was another gold digger, another woman out to get her hands on his father's money.

He ought to be accustomed to being used by now, but it always managed to surprise him. More to the point, he should've kept Hannah as an online fling, but talking to her had become too easy. She was sassy but sweet. When he talked, she listened. Really listened. That the sex was so hot as well had him hooked. Exactly why he was here and what had him shaking in his shoes at the thought she might have lied about herself. If he was right, he had to wonder why. Did she have something to hide?

Then again, he wasn't one to talk. He had secrets of his own. He hadn't told Hannah about his family, nor had he told her about Ethan. He had a thirteen-year-old son he didn't know, the result of teenage hormones. The boy was his greatest pride and the cause of his deepest regret. The birth mother had given him up for adoption. Cade had seen him once, the day he was born, and although his adoptive mother sent pictures and letters, his son had no idea who Cade was. His biggest regret in life was not fighting harder to keep him. He was terrified that if he told Hannah the truth, she'd turn around and walk away. They might not have much more than an online fling, but he needed it. He needed her.

Deciding he had to know whether or not that was Hannah, he

fished his phone from his pocket and drew up Hannah's number from his favorites. Yeah. He'd had her number for all of a week now, and she was in his favorites already. The first ring sounded across the courtyard. The woman's cheeks blazed bright red. As she fished her phone out of her back pocket, her hands shook so much it slipped from her grasp onto the ground. As she bent to retrieve it, the odd jingle sounded again and heads turned.

She punched something on the screen and held the phone to her ear. "I guess the jig's up, huh?"

A full-on grin spread across his mouth. Christ, he couldn't help himself. That *was* Hannah. He couldn't get ahead of himself, though. She had some questions to answer first. He wouldn't play the hopeless fool again, with his heart on his sleeve. "Was anything you told me true?"

She shrugged. "If I told you I was five foot three and ten pounds too heavy, would you even have met me here?"

His heart twisted. She had him there. Insecurities. He knew them well. Which meant if he expected the truth, he needed to give it as well. He had to be honest with her, even if this went nowhere.

"You don't look too heavy, baby. You look healthy. The women in my circles are too damn thin, starving themselves to meet someone else's idea of beautiful." Hannah had curves on top of curves. She had small breasts he suspected would fit perfectly in his palms, topped by strong shoulders. Her round ass filled out her dark jeans to perfection. He couldn't wait to get her out of them. He ached to discover if her skin was as soft as it looked.

"Besides, it's *you* I'm addicted to. You're the reason I go straight home to my computer at the end of every night despite swearing I was done with women seven months ago. That's the answer to your question, by the way. Why I don't find a real woman. My ex killed the need. She used me and she cheated on me, and, sadly, she wasn't the first. I found her in bed with my best friend. She used him, too, pitted us against each other for her own gain. I'm curious, though. How much of our exchanges were just you playing a game?"

He focused on his work these days. He'd had it up to his eyeballs with phony women and being used. Women who saw him as nothing more than a bank balance or a plaything had long ago worn out their welcome. His ex had been the last straw. She'd slept with Sebastian, his childhood best friend, then dropped the bomb on both of them—she was pregnant, and she didn't know which of them had fathered the child. He and his lawyer had taken her to court, forcing her to prove her claims, but so far, she hadn't complied. She was still game-playing, trying to blackmail him into paying her off.

One. That's all he wanted. One woman who'd be honest with him. Which made him wonder about Hannah.

When she didn't answer his question, he smiled, tight but polite. "I take it you did your research on me? What did you discover?"

She watched him for a moment, her gaze locked on his. Then she drew a breath, her shoulders softening. "You're a corporate lawyer. You work for your father, Declan McKenzie, in one of the largest and oldest law firms on the West Coast. Your father is worth billions and you made full partner last year, the youngest lawyer in your firm to do so. Your family also owns a small but up-and-coming software company."

He nodded. "Mmm. My sister's baby."

Impressive, but he had no desire to let her off the hook yet. She'd lied to him but shown up anyway. What was her game?

"You should have discovered by now I want the same thing you do. I want someone who can be straight with me, who doesn't see me as a means to lining their closets or stroking their inflated ego. How much of what you told me was the truth?"

Meeting Hannah had been a fluke. They'd met in an online discussion about a hot novel seated on the top of the *New York Times* bestseller list. The erotic tale had sides divided and people arguing over its BDSM aspects. He and Hannah had been arguing opposing sides of that very topic. She opposed the idea of someone *beating her*, as she'd called it. "It's barbaric!" she'd told him once. "How can beating someone turn someone on?"

His response? How would she know if she'd never tried it? Of course, forms of torture didn't arouse him. He agreed with her there. He had no desire to inflict pain on a partner. The thought of tying a woman down and having his way with her, though, made him hard enough to hammer nails, and a smack on the ass in the middle of a good groove could heighten the intensity for both of them. Which was where his turn-ons really lay—his partner's satisfaction. Watching a woman's ecstasy had to be the most erotic thing in the world, when she let go and came apart beneath him.

And so their conversation had gone. One thing led to another, and she'd admitted his ideas turned her on as well. As long as he had no plans to whip her or spank her until her behind stung so much she couldn't sit down.

"I'm sorry I didn't tell you the truth. I was afraid to. Truthfully, if you ended up like the rest of the guys I've met, I didn't want to know. I wanted to play, to be someone else for a while." Across the courtyard, another fierce blush stole across Hannah's cheeks. Her voice lowered. "I didn't lie when I told you we want the same things. I only lied about the way I look."

Apparently, she had as much to lose in this exchange as he did. "Why?"

She looked down at the ground, nudging something with the toe of her sandal. "Men want tall, thin, perfect women, with long legs and huge breasts, and as you can see, I'm not any of that."

What she *wasn't* saying hit him clear as day, and his heart twisted, his anger deflating. Someone had made her feel less than beautiful. He hated the thought.

"You look perfect from here. Your breasts look like a mouth-watering handful. Believe me, sweetheart, I'm not disappointed. If you were afraid, though, why come at all? You knew I'd discover the truth once I saw you."

She looked up, her gaze bold and unapologetic. "Because I hoped you'd be different. That you wouldn't be like all the rest."

They had the exact same fear—of being used and being judged.

"And because you're right. I had to see you."

Her last comment was the final point, making the decision for him. Having heard all he needed, Cade disconnected the call and stuffed his phone back in his pocket. Then he smiled and crooked a finger at her. She hesitated, staring at him, then hiked her chin and started across the field. His gaze transfixed on the sexy swing of her hips as she walked, and the embarrassing bulge in his slacks thickened and lengthened. How it was possible to crave someone the way he did her, he didn't know, but the reaction had been instantaneous from the first argument. Hannah had passion and it turned him the hell on.

When she stopped in front of him, the scar on her cheek came into view. The deep groove cut a jagged path from temple to chin, bisecting her right cheek. Another two-inch scar cut across her left eyebrow and a smaller one-inch slash sat below her left cheekbone.

"You didn't tell me about these." He traced the longest scar with the pad of his thumb, his chest aching with the thought of how she'd gotten them. What could cause a scar like that? No sooner had the question formed than possibilities filled his mind, and his gut knotted for the pain she must have endured. He prayed she hadn't been attacked.

She stiffened and jerked her head to the left. A curtain of hair fell forward over her shoulder, hiding her face. She folded her arms, and he got the distinct impression she meant the action to shut him out. "I suppose it's a deal breaker, then?"

Her stiff posture nudged something in his gut. Her unyielding tone told him she'd taken her question as fact.

He dropped his hand and arched a brow. "Has it ever been?"

She shrugged, offhanded and dismissive, but her stiff posture answered the question even before her response left her mouth. Someone had hurt her.

"Once or twice. I've been teased, stared at, and gossiped about enough to know this sort of thing bothers some people. The scars are deep and all the makeup in the world can't hide them. On top of the lies I told you, I wouldn't blame you if you change your mind."

Disappointment surged through him and his heart clenched. So she'd dealt with them, too, those shallow people who couldn't see beyond their own noses. A wave of anger followed on its heels. Somebody had made her believe she wasn't beautiful the way she was, and it pissed him off.

Knowing she wouldn't believe him, he set out to prove he wasn't like the other men in her life.

"We all have our secrets. I have my own, and when the time is right, I'll share them." He had to admit the thought of telling her about Ethan made his stomach tighten. Would she judge him for the choices he'd made all those years ago? Any other time, he might have kept the secret to himself. After all, their relationship was temporary, little more than a fling. But she'd shared with him. He had to give her the same trust in return. He didn't, however, want to do it now.

Her gaze darted in his direction, but the mistrust didn't disappear from her face, and she didn't otherwise move. He was going to have to prove it to her.

Decision made, he slid his hands onto her hips and over the curve of her behind, pulling her into him. Despite her clear mistrust, she went willingly. To passersby, it would look like an embrace, like a man greeting his girlfriend, but he arched his hips, pushing his straining erection into the softness of her stomach enough that she could feel it. He needed her to know he found her beautiful, and he could think of only one way to do it, given the nature of their relationship.

Hannah gasped. His breath halted as his entire body focused on hers. He'd fantasized so many times about this moment, when he'd have her in his arms. Now he had her and he couldn't concentrate worth a damn. At least not about anything except the desperate desire to drag her back to his hotel room and sink into her velvet heat. He wanted to get to know every inch of her skin, her every reaction, and he yearned to bring her more pleasure than she'd ever had.

Managing to find his brain again, he leaned his head beside her ear. A soft, lavender scent wafted over him. He had the overwhelming desire to search out every spot she'd dabbed the luscious scent. "See what you to do me? Does this feel like a man who's disappointed by what he sees? The thought of meeting you has had me hard all day, but this particular erection is from watching you walk across the courtyard. Do you have any idea how sexy your ass swings when you walk or how phenomenal you look in those jeans?"

She drew in a shuddering breath. Her stiff posture softened, and she leaned into him. "For what it's worth, I didn't know who you were until you told me. We agreed to no names, nothing to identify each other by, remember? It's part of the rules I live by. Truth is, your money doesn't mean a whole lot to me. Money pays the bills, but it can't buy happiness. Or love."

He had to admit she impressed him. She might have lied about certain aspects of herself, but he could understand why. He'd done the same.

"I agree. I might have been born into it, but I work hard for every penny. I earned my position. My father didn't hand it to me. In fact, he made me work harder because of it, made me prove myself to the other partners in the firm." Unable to help himself, he raked his teeth over her earlobe, then soothed the bite with a stroke of his tongue. "Are you wet, Hannah?"

Her fingers curled around his biceps, where she held on to him. A soft shiver ran through her. "Very."

He groaned, shoved a hand into his pocket and rearranged his erection so as not to embarrass himself, then forced himself to release her. He took her hand instead, threading his fingers through hers. It scared the hell out of him, too, how right her hand felt in his. "Let's go find that coffee. Before I drag you to a bathroom somewhere."

As they started to walk, she looked over at him, one brow arched in challenge. "Would you?"

"Oh, I would."

He halted and tugged on her hand, pulling her close enough to lean his mouth beside her ear again. He shouldn't, but he couldn't resist teasing her. She responded, and he loved that she did. She wasn't fake about it, either, which told him a lot about her character and filled his mind with fantasies. Getting to watch her reactions in person, rather than having to imagine them, had proven a lure too strong to deny.

"I'd turn you around and fuck you from behind. If I remember right, you like it from behind. I'd enjoy watching your face in the mirror. That's why I'm really here. Words on a screen aren't enough anymore. We have the same kink, sweetheart. I enjoy watching, too, and I'm dying to see the heat in your eyes when I slide into you. Hear you moan my name when you come and feel your pussy tighten around my cock."

He knew he'd hit his mark when she let out a sound that was half gasp, half moan.

"I have no desire, though, for my first time with you to be fast and furious. I intend to take my time." He nipped her earlobe, delighted in the soft shudder that went through her, then forced himself to release her. He took her hand again and resumed his trek, heading for the light on the corner. "Come on. Let's go find that coffee. I passed a Starbucks on the way from my hotel."

* * *

She couldn't stop staring at him. Seated across the small round table in Starbucks, Hannah couldn't keep her eyes off Cade. She couldn't stop herself from soaking in every detail of his tall, broad form. She'd searched him out online, found his picture on his company's website, so she knew what to expect before coming today, but seeing him in person didn't do him justice. Cade McKenzie looked like he'd stepped off the cover of *GQ* magazine. He stood a good head above her five foot three inches. Thick, broad shoulders tapered to lean hips and powerful thighs that even the perfect fit of his tailored slacks couldn't hide.

He kept his black hair short, the bristles of his bangs dabbed with a bit of gel to make them stand up. His eyes were a beautiful shade of deep green, like the moss so rampant around these parts. They seemed to catch her every move, something working in the depths that told her Cade didn't miss a thing. Coffee cups in hand, they'd sat in silence for several minutes. People occupied every table in the café around them, with five or six people waiting in the various lines inside. So far, since he'd told her he wanted her, neither had said anything. They'd walked in aching silence.

She looked down at her cup and sipped at her coffee. "Your silence is making me crazy. Tell me what you're thinking."

Cade sat back in his seat, coffee cup cradled in his large hands. "Am I what you expected?"

She lifted her gaze, surprised by the question. It screamed of insecurities. With looks like his, she wouldn't have thought he had any.

She had to be honest, though, especially if she expected the same in return. Besides, she owed it to him. "No. You don't look anything like I imagined you would and much better than the picture on your company's website. You're a walking contradiction. Your Gchat username and your views on spanking had me picturing some hot bad boy in leather, who rode a cycle and would try to convince me to be his next submissive."

He grinned at this, revealing straight, blinding white teeth. "I'm not a dom, but I do ride. Just not all the time. When I'm working, it's not practical or professional. I save my Harley for the weekends."

She bit her lower lip. He really did have a Harley. A man on a motorcycle was sexy. The thought of Mr. GQ over there on one? Damn.

She sipped her coffee, the liquid sweet and rich, warming her already-heated belly. "When I looked you up and discovered you were a rich corporate lawyer, I expected buttoned up and stuffy, full suit, and yet I see you have a tattoo."

She nodded at his left arm, resting on the table. What looked to be the tail end of either a snake or black dragon coiled up his forearm, disappearing beneath the rolled-up sleeve of his white shirt. Tattoos on a man were sexy. His contradicted the tame image that had formed in her mind when she'd done her research on him.

He arched a brow. "Is that a deal breaker?"

He'd tossed her question back at her. The hidden insecurity here as well filled her with more questions. *We all have our secrets.* He'd told her that earlier. She was dying to ask, but he'd also told her he'd share when he was ready, and she had to respect that. She understood too well the need to be sure you could really trust someone before you spilled all your secrets.

She sat up straight and held his gaze. "No. If you can handle mine, I can handle yours."

He chuckled, a low sexy rumble that made her stomach do somersaults, and heat filled his eyes, mixing with a pleased sort of amusement.

"Can you now?" He leaned forward, reached across the table, and held out his hand, palm up.

She hesitated, afraid to touch him again. The way he affected her, especially in person, was disconcerting. Here, too, though, the pull of him was irresistible, and she set her hand in his.

He studied her face as he encased her hand in his much larger palm. His thumb caressed the inside of her wrist, setting fire to her skin. "Actually, your scar caught my attention. I wondered about your reaction."

Disappointment surged through her. She stiffened and snatched her hand back, curling it around her cup. Here it came. The point where he made his excuse. "What about it?"

Cade frowned, irritation crossing his features, and he reached across the table, taking her hand back.

"You're beautiful, Hannah. Don't ever let anyone tell you otherwise. If you want the truth, I was sitting here looking at you. Up until now, I've only had my imagination to go by. It's kind of nice to be able to see you." His expression softened. "No, I wondered how you got the scars. Something like that had to be painful. You weren't attacked, were you?"

The painful memories rose faster than she could stop them. She'd sat in that car for hours, trapped in the twisted metal, watching her parents die. She'd heard her father's last breath. He'd spent hours breathing only periodically. Taking a breath, then not breathing for what often had felt like eternity, only to draw another one. He'd had a gurgle, too, and his voice had taken on a breathy wheeze as he told her he loved her for the last time. Her mother hadn't moved or spoken at all. She'd later been told her mother had died on impact.

Hannah shook her head. "I don't want to talk about it."

The intensity of his gaze as he studied her again made her hands shake, but just as suddenly, he rose from his seat and came around to her side of the table. He held his hand out. "Walk with me?"

The quiet sincerity in his gaze had her hand slipping into his. He wasn't at all what she'd expected him to be. He might have more money than she'd ever see and he might very well belong on the cover of *GQ* magazine, but he had his own insecurities. It humbled her and calmed the nervous skip of her pulse.

She rose from her chair, picked up her coffee cup, and nodded. They left the small café, stopping on the corner to wait for the light. She darted a glance at him. "Where are we going?"

He shrugged halfheartedly and darted a sidelong glance at her. "Nowhere in particular. There are too many ears at the café. If this is going to happen, we need to be comfortable with each other. Maybe if we spend some time together, we'll both relax a little."

"You're not. Comfortable, I mean."

The light changed, the green "walk" sign blinking from across the street, and Cade stepped out into the crosswalk, pulling her along with him. "Neither are you with me. You know an awful lot about me, and I don't even know your last name. Trust goes both ways, sweetheart."

He had a point. A big one.

"Not true. I've confessed quite a lot to you over the last six months. You know I'm not fond of spanking, but the thought of fucking you in public turns me on. You also know I'm a nerd. I like to read. I don't usually volunteer that stuff, because I'm a private kind of girl." As they stepped up onto the curb again and traffic resumed behind them, Hannah followed until they were out of the way of the street corner and once more back where they'd begun. She halted at the edge of the grass, forcing him to stop along with her. "Miller."

He turned to face her, brow arched, but remained silent. Hannah drew a breath.

"My full name is Hannah Renee Miller. I own a bookstore downtown here. A couple blocks over. We sell new and used books, but my specialty is finding the rare ones. I read that erotic book because people kept coming in and asking for it. I decided to find out what all the hubbub was about."

She looked down at the grass. An exposed feeling crept over her. She needed to bare a wound, for the sake of being honest with him, and it never came easy.

"The scars are from a car accident. My parents died a little after my fourteenth birthday. We were hit by a drunk driver on the way home from a school play I was in. My mother died on impact.

I listened to my father stop breathing. Then spent three hours alone with them until another car finally passed and stopped. I spent a week in the hospital. With no immediate family, they put me into the foster care system."

Sadness filled his eyes and his fingers tightened around hers. "I'm sorry about your parents. That must have been very painful."

"Thank you."

He flashed a lopsided grin. "Was that so hard?"

She blew out a defeated breath but couldn't resist a grin.

"Yes." Her smile fell. "I don't talk about it much, because it's still painful. I grew up taking care of myself. You and I come from different worlds. It honestly makes me nervous, because I can't see what someone like you would want in someone like me. I lied about my looks because I didn't want to know if my scars would bother you. Take a look at any magazine and you'll discover what most men consider attractive. I told you. I'm not any of that."

Now she'd done it. He'd run for sure now.

Cade, however, did the exact opposite of what she expected. He tugged her close, releasing her hand to slip his around her waist. His tall, broad body hit hers, warm and solid, and Hannah froze. When he bent his head, she held her breath. God, he was going to kiss her.

His mouth whispered across hers, working into a luscious tangle of lips and tongues. Something about it unknotted her stomach. His kiss called to a primal place within her, calling to that lonely woman inside who needed everything he represented, and she couldn't help herself. She lifted onto her toes to complete the connection, needing more of him. Someone let out a quiet groan, though she couldn't be certain who.

She only knew he'd effectively swept her off her feet. The man made kissing an art form. She hadn't been certain what to expect. He'd always been laid-back and reserved, strong but content to let her take the lead. She'd liked that about him. So far, they seemed in a similar position—both holding back out of fear of something.

He gave her the same sense of power withheld now. His kiss melted her defenses. His lips slid over hers, and she tilted her head, opening for him. Her knees wobbled and her free hand sought the solid warmth of his body. She pressed her breasts into his hard chest, desperate for the friction of her nipples rubbing his skin.

A car honked somewhere in the street nearby, jerking Hannah back to reality. They were in public. She pulled her mouth from his but could only stare at him, breathless.

He wrapped his arm tighter around her and pulled her hard against him. His erection pushed into her stomach, solid as steel. Both of them were shaking.

After a moment, he opened his eyes, those mossy depths once again burning into her. The hunger there left her breathless. "My hotel's only a few blocks from here."

His statement was subtle, but it hit her low, setting a blaze burning in her stomach. Something moved between them, indescribable, yet there all the same. The memory of all those nights. The erotic chats they'd shared. The promise of the night before them. Oh, for sure he wanted her the way she wanted him, and the thought of his hands on her skin had her trembling all over again, partly in fear. Once he caught sight of the scars on her torso, though, would he still want her?

When she didn't answer, he leaned his forehead against hers. "Tell me you want me as much as I want you."

The need and the subtle vulnerability in his voice washed away everything else and made her brave. She hadn't come today to let fear stop her from enjoying him. He was sexy and sweet and Maddie was right. If she didn't do this, take this step into the first reckless relationship she'd ever had, she'd regret it. She'd end up where she'd already been—at home, alone.

She pressed closer, rocking her hips into his. "Lead the way."

Chapter Three

Hannah's nerve endings were shredded as they walked. Even her knees wobbled. The four blocks to Cade's hotel passed in an aching silence. The air between them filled with the luscious promise of things to come. The rest of the city around her faded as her senses honed in on the man beside her. His large presence. The scent of him that seemed to float on the breeze blowing past her. Even his long, purposeful stride did naughty things to her insides.

It didn't help that he kept glancing at her. When his gaze collided with hers—because she couldn't stop looking at him, either—the hunger burning there made her stomach do somersaults.

The simple touch of his hand in hers seemed intimate and set fire to her insides. He had the hands of a man who'd never done a day of manual labor in his life, who sat behind a desk all day. They were smooth and uncalloused. His thumb kept stroking her fingers in an idle fashion. The simple touch made her yearn to have those large, smooth hands on *her*. All over her.

She hadn't had sex in over a year, hadn't had *wild* sex in…well, okay, ever. She was about to spend time with a man whose hand in hers made her panties damp. Whispers of their previous chats flitted through her mind. They always generated so much heat between them. Would it be the same in person? Her entire body buzzed with the yearning to find out.

Several minutes later, they stood together in the quiet hallway outside his suite. Of course he stayed at the best of the best. The five-star accommodation screamed luxury in every small detail, from the doorman dressed in formal attire, who greeted them on the way in, to the sweeping staircase in the lobby. The place resembled a mansion, done in classic décor from marble flooring to draperies on the windows. His room alone no doubt cost more than her shop grossed in a month.

As he inserted the keycard in the door, her stomach tied itself in knots. Was she ready to do this? Online, they were equals, but here, in this expensive hotel, she was out of place, and Cade was far, far out of her league. She felt like a poor peasant girl to his Prince Charming.

The lock mechanism clicked and Cade pushed the handle, shoving the door. As he held it open, he turned to face her and smiled, wicked and mischievous. "There's time to back out, you know."

Hannah forced a laugh to cover the unease gripping her by the throat.

Apparently, her laugh sounded as phony as it felt, for Cade's smile fell. Gaze somber, he lifted his left hand, stroking his thumb over her chin. "You okay?"

She wanted to laugh it off, but she'd lied to him enough. The second time around, she gave him a more honest smile, though it still wobbled a bit. "I'm nervous."

His fingers tightened in hers. "Mmm. Me too."

The quiet tone of his voice caught her, filling her with questions. "May I ask why? You don't look it."

Cade pushed the door open fully and pulled her inside the suite. She barely registered the click of the door falling shut before his large, warm hands slid into her hair. A bare breath later, he pressed her back against an adjacent wall.

"Because I've been dying to do this." He covered her mouth with his, and any thought of being nervous flew right out the window.

The kiss on the street had been sweet, a taste, passion withheld. The kiss of two people trying each other out for the first time. This one was a hot brand. It promised pleasure lay in her future. His tongue traced the seam of her lips, a question and a tease in one hot stroke. When she opened on a soft sigh, he plunged inside, his tongue dueling with hers. Goose bumps chased each other over the surface of her skin.

If his kiss alone weren't enough to overwhelm her senses, his hands moved, stroking over her. Down her sides, over her hips to her butt, only to move back up her stomach and skimming the underside of her breasts. His body surrounded her, blocking out everything but him, and Hannah let herself get lost. She sought him out as well, feeling over his firm pecs to his flat abdomen. She yearned to discover the hard muscle and warm skin beneath the fabric of his shirt. Yearned to discover all those luscious places that would drive him mad, make him gasp and groan. She wanted to remember every tiny detail for when he eventually went back to San Diego and she lay alone in the dark, craving exactly this.

"I've been dying to get my hands on you." His voice rumbled against her skin as his lips skimmed across her jaw and down her neck. "Do you know how torturous it is to be so turned on by someone you can't even see? You have a way with words, Miss Miller."

His use of her name had a shiver running over the surface of her skin. She yearned to hear him call her name in the grip of an orgasm. Her hips pushed forward, seeking contact with his body. When the softness of her belly brushed the hard bulge in his pants, she couldn't contain a moan.

He nipped at her bottom lip, then pulled back and took her hand. "Come on. Before I fuck you against this wall."

The thought was damn tempting, but he wasn't the only one who wanted to take his time. If she had only this one night with him, she intended to make the most of it.

"Uh-uh." Hannah planted her feet, and he stopped, looking back, uncertainty in his gaze.

Rather than tell him, she moved around him and led him farther inside. As it turned out, Cade's suite came complete with its own living room and a tiny little kitchen, all done in the same extravagant, old mansion style décor. The place awed her. Her entire apartment had less space than this room.

She led him to the couch, then released his hand and pointed. "I want to take my time with you as well. Sit."

He grinned and did as she asked, sinking onto the couch, then crooking a finger at her. Standing over him, Hannah shoved her shy, quiet side into the closet and locked the door. Something about his expression filled her with feminine power. If he minded her scar, it didn't show, and she wanted to take advantage, to let it fuel her desires and set her free.

She wanted to enjoy him, and she wouldn't let her insecurities keep her from doing so. Empowered by the thought, she climbed into his lap, straddling him. His hands warmed her skin even through the thick material of her jeans as he slid them up her thighs. He didn't, however, lean in to kiss her. His expression grew serious, his green gaze raking over her face. Was he really that nervous? Once again, the thought humbled her.

She sat back on his knees and settled a hand against his chest. "What?"

His hands stilled, curving around the tops of her thighs. "Before this goes any further, I need to say one thing."

She nodded. "All right."

"If you're looking for permanent, I'm not it. This"—he gestured between them with his index finger—"is all about sex. No doubt incredible sex, but *just* sex. This doesn't go beyond this room."

She suppressed a grin. His fumbling words ought to offend her, but the emotion wouldn't come. Rather, they spoke to her and bared his heart. In this instance, she and Cade had a lot in common. She had the same fears, so hearing him lay his on the table made her feel closer to him. Whether he meant to or not, his rule told her a lot about him. Someone had used him as well. "I'm surprised at you, GQ."

He cocked a brow. "GQ?"

This time, she couldn't help smiling.

"You look like you stepped off the cover of a *GQ* magazine."

She smoothed a hand over the curve of one bulging bicep and across his chest. "I'm betting you work out every day."

He stiffened beneath her, a shadow of something passing over his face, there and carefully masked again before she caught what it had been. "I'm expected to keep up certain appearances."

His hardened expression screamed of secrets hidden and painful disappointments. She couldn't stop the echo of hurt from moving through her. The questions formed on her tongue, but she bit them back. They weren't here for love. She shouldn't care, and them getting to know each other more than necessary would end in her getting attached. That was dangerous, because in the end, everybody left. What she'd liked about their online exchanges was the anonymity. She hadn't known him and thus couldn't care or become attached or wait for him to decide he was through with her. Because it didn't matter. They used each other.

She stiffened her spine, remembering her role. "Well, I have to admit I expected a bit more finesse coming from a man whose job it is to sway people's opinion."

He held her gaze, bold and unapologetic, but the nervous edge had yet to leave his eyes. His hand trembled as he smoothed it up her thigh. "I'm sorry. When I'm nervous I tend to revert to what's comfortable. I'm used to presenting the facts, cold and blunt."

Determined to relax him, she fisted his red tie and tugged on the end. "Does that speech always work to woo the ladies?"

The left corner of his mouth quirked, but the smile fell as quickly as it came. His big hands caressed over the curve of her hips and up her back. "I wouldn't know. I've never said it to anyone else before."

This caught her. He drew clear boundary lines, and she wanted to ask what made her so special. In that moment, though, vulnerability hung all over him. The anxiousness screaming from his gaze told her he was out of his element. Once again, he reminded her how different he was from the image he'd portrayed online. In the flesh, he was every bit as flawed and human as she was. Seeing his human frailty filled her with more questions and nudged something inside, but she shoved the queries aside. In another lifetime, he might have been someone she'd want to get to know better. In another lifetime, maybe they'd lie together in the dark and share wounds.

Gaze downcast, she forced her mind to focus on the task at hand and worked at undoing the knot in his tie. Like he said, they were here for sex, nothing more, nothing less. She had no desire to date him or get her heart broken again. "Trust goes both ways, GQ. If it makes you feel any better, your money doesn't mean much to me. Do your research, the same way I did on you. You'll find enough to know I am who I say I am. I've been taking care of myself since I was fourteen. No offense, but I *don't* need you."

The corners of his mouth twitched, amusement gleaming in his eyes. "I appreciate that, thanks."

Tie undone, she whipped it from around his neck and dropped it to the floor beside the couch.

"I have a few rules of my own. I agree. I don't want hearts and flowers, either. I want to use you for a while." She arched a brow. "You okay with that?"

His hands slid to her backside. He pulled her tight against the ridge of his erection, straining the front placket of his black pants. "You tell me."

She gasped. The solid press of his cock against her core, against the spot that had been throbbing for a week now, overwhelmed her system. Since they'd made plans to meet, she'd been in a state of constant arousal. She'd given herself so many orgasms in the last week while fantasizing about this exact moment she ought to have gotten it out of her system by now. Yet a hot, luscious pulse shot straight to her clit. She wanted him, too.

She let out a quiet, shuddering breath but held tight to her composure. "This is just for one night. Whether we go back to what we were remains to be seen, but I don't want to do this again."

Okay, so she lied. She had a feeling she could do this with him again. And again. And again. He was right on one account. Their exchanges had become intense. She'd become addicted, too.

Cade leaned forward, scraping his teeth over her bottom lip. "I'd like to negotiate that. I'm going to be here for two weeks. I don't see why we can't enjoy each other while I'm here."

His hands slid up her torso to curve around each breast, his velvet lips wandering along her chin and down the side of her neck. Hannah forgot her name, let alone any form of protest. Her fingers curled of their own volition into the hard muscle of his broad shoulders.

She closed her eyes, desperate to hold on to what little sanity she had left. Heated tremors ran the length of her spine. "And I w-won't spend the n-night. I have a job, and I need to be fresh in the morning."

The bookstore was an excuse and a lousy one. Falling asleep in someone's arms created things like intimacy, and she knew better.

He nipped at the spot where her neck met her shoulder. "Ditto."

She lifted her head and opened her eyes, pulling away enough to look into his face. Now came the serious stuff. His answer to her next question would tell her about the man and could make or break their night altogether. She wouldn't be somebody's joke again.

His playful expression fell, his brows drawing together in concern. "What is it?"

She stiffened her spine, determined to get the words out. Her hands shook so much she feared he'd feel her trembling. Nausea swirled in her stomach. "I also need to be the only person you're sleeping with. What you do in your own time is your business, but while you're here, I won't be one in a long line of your conquests, or a joke between you and another woman."

The heat of the moment before faded, seriousness taking its place between them. He sat back, his green gaze working over her face in disbelief. "Have you ever?"

Embarrassed heat rose up her neck and into her cheeks. She glanced down at their combined laps, staring at the creases in his slacks, and nodded. "Somebody played a cruel joke once, my freshman year in college."

"Well, he was an asshole." He cupped her face in his hands and forced her gaze back to his, his thumbs sweeping her cheeks. "That won't be a problem. To be honest, I'm not intimate with anybody but you in any way, shape, or form. Up until seven months ago, I dated a woman I thought I wanted to spend the rest of my life with."

His words caught her. It meant, for all intents and purposes, Cade McKenzie was the marrying type. The wounded little girl inside her pulsed to life. Deep down, in a place she didn't want to name or face, she wanted the fantasy, the one all little girls dreamed of. A man she could trust, who'd spend the rest of his life worshiping her. So far, life had proven Prince Charming didn't exist. Better to stay uninvolved.

She ran her finger around one of the buttons on his shirt. "The woman who cheated on you."

Something flashed across his features, but his expression went impassive again before she grasped what the emotion had been.

"Mmm. I found out she wanted what every woman I've dated seems to want."

"The money." She laid a hand against his chest. She may not understand this specific pain, but she knew what it meant to be used. "I'm sorry."

He made a noncommittal grunt in the back of his throat. "Since the breakup, I haven't dated. I guess you could say I've lost my desire to do so. I didn't plan what developed between you and me. You had such strong opinions of the book that I enjoyed challenging you."

She couldn't help smiling. "So did I."

He rubbed slow, soothing circles over her back. "I didn't expect to like you or for this to lead where it did. So, no worries, babe. You're it for me."

His quiet admission relaxed the last of her nerves. They had a lot in common. They'd both arrived at the same place in their lives, both needing a connection but not wanting the heartache that came with relationships. Staring at him, he no longer seemed a stranger anymore, but the man she'd come to know over the last few months. Whose words on a computer screen could light up her whole day.

His earlier words filled her mind. Before this went any further, she might as well know now. "You said you had secrets. Anything I should know?"

His gaze worked over her face, searching as if something weighed on him. Finally, he drew a breath and that vulnerability returned to his eyes. "Yes, but…not now."

The smart girl who'd been hurt one time too many insisted she ought to know everything before she got involved with him. It was the anxiousness in the depths of his eyes, though, that told her she already knew. "It's painful."

"Not quite like your accident, but it's not easy to talk about and it sends my head into places I don't want to go right now." A ghost of a smile whispered across his mouth, humor flaring in his gaze. "I don't want to ruin the moment. I promise it's nothing bad, at least not for you. I will tell you. Just not now."

She nodded, stroking a reassuring hand over his chest. "All right."

Relief flooded his features and his body relaxed beneath her.

"Thank you. So…" He sat back, hands on her hips, and cocked a playful brow. "Any more demands, Miss Miller?"

Filled with a sense of freedom, she let go of her inhibitions and leaned forward, pressing her chest to his. "No, that's it. For now."

"Good." He caught her bottom lip in his teeth, then soothed the soft bite with a stroke of his tongue. His voice lowered to a husky murmur between them. "Now tell me what you want. Did you notice the bed?"

She turned, following his gaze. Double doors leading to the bedroom stood open, revealing a huge behemoth of a bed, decorated with no less than six pillows and a fluffy quilt. The gorgeous, four-poster bed lined the wall, deep mahogany in color with a carved wooden frame.

Cade leaned forward, his voice a low, sexy rumble in her ear. "I booked this room on purpose. At some point, I'm going to tie you to it and show you what I meant about restraints. There's also a fantastic tub I want to get you in at some point. For now, however, I've decided to let you lead."

She braced her hands against his chest and pushed upright.

"We'll negotiate the bed later. For starters, I want this shirt off. I want to see the rest of your tattoo." She slid off his lap and moved to the small, overstuffed chair, catty-corner to the couch. She shifted the chair, turning it to face the couch, and sat.

Hands already making quick work of the buttons on his shirt, he shifted forward, as if he were about to get up.

Hannah shook her head and held up a hand. "Uh-uh. Stay. I want to watch."

Cade's fingers paused over the next button. He stared for a moment before comprehension dawned across his face. He sank back into the couch cushions with a groan. "Baby, I didn't come all the way out here to touch myself. I can stay home and do that."

She arched a brow. "You recall me telling you my biggest fantasy?"

He let out a frustrated growl. "I've tried several times to fulfill it, but you wouldn't ever let me see you."

She smiled again. "Take off your shirt, Cade."

"You're a bossy little thing." He grinned but freed another button. "What happened to shy Hannah?"

Her smile fell, the playful pretense for a moment forgotten. The air of seriousness returned as unease rose over her. "I feel comfortable with you. I hadn't expected it, all things considered, but I do."

He returned her smile, this one soft and understanding. "Me too."

A sense of mutual respect passed between them, tender and hot at the same time. Cade had become her friend, her lover. His smile told her he shared the sentiment.

She craved that about their exchanges, about him, the most. It had never been just sex, but something more. They shared a connection. Something about him warmed her insides. He seemed familiar and something in her always melted beneath the power of it. She couldn't put a name to the emotion. She refused to ponder it, but for tonight at least, she'd give in. She needed him too much. Tonight, she wanted to feel like a woman, desired and beautiful.

He grinned, once again playful and mischievous, and nodded in her direction. "If I have to get naked, so do you. Shirt. Off. I want to see you."

The heat flaring in his gaze made her obey, but it didn't escape her notice that he hadn't asked. He'd demanded.

The corners of her mouth twitched with her effort to hold back a grin. "You're used to getting your way, aren't you?"

Two buttons down, his fingers once again halted. He grinned, his eyes glittering with playful impishness. "Yes, ma'am. Now do as you're told and take off your shirt."

Unable to resist the playful tease, she gripped the hem of her shirt and lifted it enough to reveal her belly, then arched a brow at him. "You first."

He made quick work of the rest of the buttons, pulled

his shirt out from beneath the waistband of his slacks, and shrugged out of it, then balled it and tossed it at her. It landed on her feet with a soft swish of fabric, still warm from the heat of his body.

"Ball's in your court now, baby." He sat back, folding his hands over his bare stomach. A nice flat stomach dusted with a smattering of dark hair. She preferred guys who looked like men, not little boys, but who also didn't resemble wildebeests. Cade had just the right amount covering his well-defined pecs. Her fingers itched to dive into the dark curls.

Her gaze shifted, falling to his tattoo. A black snakelike dragon ran from his shoulder to the middle of his forearm. Classy and simple, nothing garish, but it made a bold statement. Unable to help herself, she rose from her seat and moved to stand beside the couch.

"I like this." She followed the dragon's body with the tip of a finger as it wound its way up his arm.

He glanced at his shoulder and shrugged. "Call it an act of rebellion. It goes with that story I'll tell you sometime. I got it when I turned eighteen. It pissed off my father. My parents have certain expectations for my sister and I. Everything we've ever done has been dictated to us, and I wanted to unseat the old man."

He'd mentioned a sister before. She looked up, finger pausing on a stroke over the dragon's serpentlike tongue. "You have a sister?"

"Mmm. I'm a twin, though she's fond of telling people she's older." The corners of his mouth twitched, amusement filling his gaze.

"Does she look like you?" She shouldn't have asked him that, but the mention of his family reminded her how much she didn't know about him, other than what she'd gleaned online. They didn't talk about this side of themselves. She was about to become intimate with a man whose words could make her come so hard she lost her breath, but she didn't know his family or his life. His innocent sharing filled her with a dangerous yearning to know more. She ached to learn about his world, to see the *man*.

"We look like siblings. I'm told she looks like a smaller, feminine version of me." He reached over, fingering the hem of her shirt. "I don't want to talk about my sister. I want to talk about you taking this off."

He cocked a brow and waited, but her nerves were getting the best of her. Truth was, she'd stalled on purpose. What could she tell him? Despite having been the one to initiate this, the thought of baring her not-so-perfect body still made her stomach churn. Having to stand in front of him and watch his every reaction made her limbs shake. She had a running nightmare she'd make a dork out of herself and get stuck in her shirt. Or she'd take it off and have to watch the revulsion rise in his eyes.

He dropped his head against the back of the couch.

"I'm hanging on a thread, baby. I'm about three seconds from standing up and taking it off myself." Despite the playful threat, he spoke softly, his fingers wandering beneath the hem of her shirt, stroking over her trembling belly. "For months I've had nothing but my imagination to go by. Here you are in front of me. I *need* to see you. All of you."

The hunger in his eyes encouraged her. She let it fuel her own hunger and gripped the hem of her shirt, pulling it off over her head. She dropped it to the floor, then did the same with her tank top. Wearing only her bra, she waited, heart going gangbusters in her throat.

Cade growled low as he slid his hand up her belly. His fingers grazed the underside of her left breast, encased in the red, lacy bra. His hot gaze trapped her, an all-too-willing prisoner.

Feeling braver now, she shook her head and moved to the overstuffed chair but didn't take a seat. His gaze followed her every move as she unbuttoned her jeans and slid them down her hips. She stepped out of them, pushing them aside with her foot, and stood before him in the matching bra and panties she'd bought for this date. A red number she'd hoped would match his tie. She was pleased to see it did.

Hands trembling, she let him look at her for a moment, then sat in the chair. Gaze locked on his, she leaned back and ran her hand down her stomach and over her lace-covered mound, rubbing herself through her panties. "Your turn."

His chest rose and fell at an increasingly rapid pace, his hands visibly shaking as he undid his belt. He unzipped his slacks and reached inside, pulling out his cock, then sat back. Hannah licked her lips. He was beautiful, long and thick, the head stretching up his stomach to touch his belly button. She wasn't certain what she wanted more…to climb on his lap and sink onto him or take him in her mouth. The unbearable need to taste him warred with the fantasy they'd been playing out for too many months. To watch him stroke himself to orgasm. To get to watch his face when he came.

He wrapped his hand around the head and squeezed, eyes fluttering closed and mouth falling open in bliss. He stroked himself once, twice, then opened his heavy-lidded eyes again. "The rest. Please. I want to see all of you."

Hannah bit her lower lip and did as he asked, unable to stop her gaze from soaking in the sight he made. She had to admit it. Watching him sitting there, gaze locked on her, filled her with a sense of power. Cade McKenzie had a beautiful body, every inch of him lean and sculpted. For tonight at least, he was all hers.

She tossed her bra to the floor and massaged her breasts, caressing them and pinching the nipples, then moved to her panties. She teased him, pulled them halfway down, then back up, before turning her back to him and bending over as she pushed them down her legs. She wiggled her backside at him then turned back around and took a seat in the chair.

Cade banged his head against the back of the couch. The tendons in his neck strained. His jaw tightened. His hand stroked his cock slow but steady. "Christ, you're killing me. *Please*. I'm *dying* to touch you."

She shook her head, and he let out another growl, this one loud and frustrated. His hand squeezed his cock, the head purple and swollen. Her effect on him filled her with an addicting sense of power. She had the sense right then she could do anything. No man had ever looked at her with that much desire or begged her in such a desperate way. It might be cruel to make him sit and watch. He was right. She hadn't met him here so she could touch herself. By God, she had to prolong this as much as possible. The expression on his face filled her with an unparalleled sense of being beautiful and powerful.

Maybe, though, the time had come to let him off the hook and be honest.

"It's addicting." Soaking in the sight of him, letting it fuel her desire and her bravery, she slid her fingers down her slit, swiping her index finger over her clit. One stroke sent a heady rush shuddering through her. She gasped, her back arching off the chair. "Watching you. God, Cade, I'm so aroused. Sitting here, knowing I do that to you. Nobody's ever looked at me the way you are right now. Like I'm…"

She shook her head, letting the words drift off. Embarrassment heated her cheeks, and she averted her gaze, focusing on the movement of his hand. She couldn't say the words.

"Beautiful." He growled the words, his voice thick and strained. "You're fucking beautiful. Anybody who tells you otherwise is an asshole who doesn't deserve you anyway. Spread your legs, baby. Let me see."

Another rush of heat raced up her neck. She had to be red as a tomato, but she did as he asked and spread her thighs, opening herself to his hot gaze. She had a feeling of being made of glass, wide open before him, and as vulnerable as a newborn baby. She'd never done this either, touched herself while a lover watched.

His eyes slid to half-mast, their heat burning through her. "I want to bury my face between your thighs. Do you know how torturous this is? Dip your fingers inside and taste yourself. Tell me what you taste like, baby. Tell me what I'm missing."

Sliding her fingers inside made her moan. Fire licked along every nerve ending, making her extra sensitive. Her gaze glued to his hand, working his cock, and instead of her fingers, she imagined the fat head sliding inside of her. Her thighs shook with the need to come. Her eyes fluttered closed. She wanted, needed, and craved more but did as he asked. She pulled her fingers out and opened her eyes, gaze locked on his as she inserted them in her mouth. "A little sweet, a hint of tangy, kind of musky."

He groaned, this one long and low, and squeezed his cock in his fist. "You're killing me. I'm so fucking close."

"Me too. So close." She let out a shuddering breath, flicking her finger back and forth over her swollen clit.

"Come for me, baby. Let it go." His voice shook, his hand working his cock faster and faster.

It took all of three strokes. Three tiny little flicks of her finger and her climax slammed into her, a series of luscious bubbles bursting inside of her. She gasped, breathless, hips arching off the chair, pushing into the pressure of her fingers. A litany of quiet moans left her mouth. All the while images of him flew through her mind, leaving her gasping yet still yearning.

Somewhere in the haze, Cade swore under his breath. She turned her head, needing to see, in time to watch him squeeze his eyes shut. The muscles of his abdomen jumped as his climax tore through him. Her pussy clenched in response. Hannah bit her lower lip. To know she could do to him what he did to her made her hot all over again.

They sat in silence, harsh breathing the only sound between them for several minutes. Cade moved first. He tucked himself back in his underwear, then rose from his seat, pants still open and hanging off his hips, and moved around the coffee table to her. Hands braced on the arms of her chair, he leaned over her and seized her mouth, kissing her hard. When she purred and leaned into him, he released her and straightened.

"Bath. I'd like to be a gentleman and pick you up and carry you in there, but I'm a mess at the moment." He winked and held out a hand, his eyes hot and hungry. When she accepted, he pulled her to her feet and leaned into her ear, raking his teeth over the lobe. "You can clean me up; then I want you. All of you. I need to feel your skin against mine and your body wrapped around me."

The hot promise of his words and the need all but screaming from his tone sent a shiver down her spine, settling warm and gooey between her thighs. She turned her head, meeting his gaze. "You aren't...*tired*?"

He chuckled and winked at her, talking as he led her around the corner into the suite's bedroom. "I've been dying to get my hands on you for months. I meant it when I said I'm addicted to you. Here you are, in the flesh. We're going to talk about the time frame, because I'm not sure one night is enough to get you out of my system. I should order food before we get in the tub, because I don't plan on getting dressed for a while."

Chapter Four

It shouldn't feel this good to hold her.

Seated behind Hannah in the two-person tub half an hour later, Cade took immense pleasure in playing with her hardening nipples. Rubbing them, pinching softly. She lay back against his chest, her head lolling on his shoulder, her hands caressing his thighs beneath the water. A comfortable companionship sat between them. The same lazy ease they'd found in their online chats had followed them here. Being with her was…easy. So far, neither had said much of anything. Words weren't necessary.

Another brush of his fingers and her breathing hitched, a soft shudder moving through her. Despite what he'd told her when he brought her in here, he'd hoped they could relax a bit. As much as he wanted her, he didn't want to rush into this. Maybe they could talk, and he'd learn something about her that would untie the knot in his chest. She held certain things back from him and it made him nervous. He'd be stupid to assume she was different from anybody else. She could be another Amelia for all he knew.

Except her curves fit against the hard planes of his body like a glove. Her soft hands on his body were a salve on a wound. He needed her to keep making that sound. He pinched her left nipple, and she gasped, dropping her head back onto his shoulder. His cock hardened against her back. He'd had an erection for days now. Everything about her aroused the hell out of him. She could be so soft and understated, yet she had a bold side that surprised him. Her curves drove him mad. Instead of the stick-thin figures of the women in his circles, she had real curves, and he wanted his hands and his cock all over every inch of her. He wanted as much of her as he could get before he had to go home, back to his lonely life. It didn't help she shivered against him like nobody had ever touched her like this before.

He nipped at her neck. "I'm trying very hard to be good and resist you, but I can't stand it. I want you too much."

Her hands stilled beneath the water. "You brought me in here for a purpose."

He trailed his lips up the side of her neck, flicking out his tongue to taste her salty skin. "Mmm. I hoped we could talk."

A shiver ran through her. "A-about?"

"You. And us. We need to finish discussing terms. You haven't told me whether or not this is for just tonight or if you agree to the two weeks."

She stiffened. "Cade…"

"But it can wait, because I can't." He let his hand wander beneath the surface of the water. He found her slippery folds, the little hot button she had her fingers all over already swollen.

When they'd agreed to meet, he hadn't anticipated the woman who'd shown up. He'd expected more of the same. A woman this side of too thin, who'd feed him a phony persona. Hannah had feminine curves he couldn't get enough of, and she was real. Her boldness made him laugh. Her vulnerability called to a protectiveness within him. He'd hoped if he could get his hands on her for real, he could get his fill of her and end the insanity. Back home, he couldn't think about anything but her and warning bells had begun to sound in his head. He liked her. Too much.

He'd been wrong. One night would never be enough. He had a feeling he could lie with her in the dark, no sex at all, and still not get enough. Now, the simple, innocent sound of her whimpers drove him mad. Her body came alive beneath his touch. It made him want to roar from the damn rooftops or beat his chest.

He circled her clit, unable to resist teasing her. When she moaned and rocked her hips forward, he plunged two fingers inside of her. As he pumped them in and out, he nibbled any part of her he could reach, her neck, her shoulder, the curve of her jaw.

"I want to be here, Hannah. So damn deep inside you. I want to know the sounds you make when it's me inside you instead of your fingers, and I want to know what you feel like clamping down around me when you come."

"God, yes." She gasped, arching her back. Her hips rocked in time with the gentle thrust of his fingers. The harder he thrust into her, the harder she pushed against his hand. He let her have the moment. He couldn't help himself. She was so damn beautiful. When the movement of her hips became a desperate jerking and her breathing grew harsh and ragged, he pulled his fingers away. When she went, he wanted to go with her, wanted to be buried deep inside of her, so he could absorb every luscious shudder.

The fingers of her left hand clamped around his thigh. "Don't stop. Please don't stop."

He nuzzled her cheek, her earlobe, all the while sliding his hands beneath her bottom. "You want me, baby?"

Her head rocked on his shoulder. "*Need*, Cade. I *need* you. Don't stop."

"What's the magic word?" It might be cruel to enjoy tormenting her as much as he did, but he couldn't help himself. Watching her was addicting, even more so than their late-night chats. Every moan or sigh or shudder only magnified his own need. He wanted to make sure she never forgot this exchange. Maybe he'd never see her again, but he wanted her to look back on her time with him and be glad it happened.

He flicked his tongue over her earlobe, then bit down softly. "Say it."

Her hips jerked, her head banging back against his shoulder. "Fuck me!"

He slid down in the tub, arched his hips, and plunged into her. He meant to tease her, but her heat clamped around him, and she thrust against him, a wild bucking that drove him beyond the boiling point. He gripped her hips, trying to hold her still, to take it slow and prolong the pleasure for both of them. God, if he came inside of her…

But she was hot and slick. She took what she wanted with abandon, used his cock to satiate her needs as if he were a toy, hers to do with as she pleased, and it was sexy as hell. Her response fueled the fire burning through him, and he lost his mind.

He thrust harder, pushing deeper. Nothing mattered but the desperate need to shove her to the edge and take her over it. The sounds of their lovemaking filled the room. Her quiet whimpers, the sloshing of the water over the sides of the tub. In no less than a dozen strokes, her body stiffened against him. A high-pitched cry tore from her throat, one he'd heard a dozen times in the last week. Her body clamped around him, and he lost his grip on what little control he'd had. His orgasm rushed up in a blinding, white-hot flash that had him moaning her name and shaking along with her.

She collapsed back on his chest, and they sat together in stunned silence. Their harsh, erratic breathing filled the space between them. As his body came down from the high, the realization slid over him, like slamming into a wall at two hundred miles an hour. The condom. He'd forgotten the condom. He'd lost his head and emptied himself inside her.

He swore under his breath, his limbs shaking for an entirely different reason. "Hannah, I…"

The rest of the words wouldn't come. Panic clawed its way through his chest. He never lost his head. He planned everything, for crying out loud, right down to their affair. He never got so lost in a woman's touch he forgot everything but her, much less important stuff like condoms. He'd learned that lesson the hard way, and not once in the last thirteen years had he ever forgotten.

Until Hannah. Twice now he'd done something out of character for him. He didn't do flings with anonymous women, either, and he certainly didn't fly to another state for the need to see them.

"It's okay." She reached back, stroking his cheek, soothing and soft, as if she understood his sudden panic. Or maybe she could read his damn mind. "I'm on the pill."

He released a breath he didn't realize he'd been holding.

Hannah turned at the waist to look back at him. Brow furrowed, her gaze darted over his face, as if she searched for something specific. She sat up and shifted in the bath, turning around and straddling his thighs. "How many times have you been used?"

Her question held a bold statement. It told him in no uncertain terms she saw him, *really* saw him, in a way no woman had in a long time. That prospect alone had his heart hammering his rib cage, but her words also showed him her heart in the process. Only someone who'd *been* used would know the ache it left inside. That she even cared told him a lot about her character and made him feel somehow closer to her.

He shouldn't tell her the truth. He should make up an excuse, talk his way out of this one. The truth left his mouth anyway. He wanted her to know where he stood, but deep down, he couldn't help himself. Talking to her had always come easy. She never judged.

"A few." He drew a deep breath and released it, the faces flitting like ghosts through his memory. "Women throw themselves at me. Most of them want me for one of two things. They either want my name and the money that comes with it, or they want me to be their arm candy. Many of the single women in my world want rich husbands to help them maintain their lavish lifestyle. Some of the older ones want toys."

She studied him for a moment, her gaze this side of worried as it worked over his face. Then a playful grin bloomed. She slid a hand down his arm, squeezing his left bicep, and winked. "Can't say I blame them there, GQ. You do make very pretty arm candy."

"Minx." He leaned forward, scraped his teeth over her shoulder, and nipped his way up the side of her neck. "Are you telling me you're using me?"

"Oh, I plan on using this body to my full advantage." She let out a little purr he found damn erotic and tipped her head to the side, giving him better access. Her hands slid down his chest, a slow, sensual slide of her slippery, wet fingers, then stopped. Her voice lowered to a vulnerable murmur between them. "Though I have no desire to show it off to anyone else."

Her unspoken claim hung in the air between them, catching Cade in that painful place in his chest. The lonely part of him that connected to her in the darkness of night, when the day had been long and he wasn't in the mood to play. When their conversations took a turn for the emotional. When he spilled his heart's desires because he couldn't help himself, because talking to her came as easily as breathing.

An air of somberness rose over the room, and he lifted his head from her throat. He had to give her this one. As his gaze met hers, the playfulness of the moment before evaporated. "I don't want you sleeping with anyone else either."

She studied him for a long moment. He'd noted the same odd, searching gaze more than once since she'd arrived an hour ago. Her gaze would skirt over his face, something working behind her eyes he could see but not gain access to. He could read people like the back of his hand, but Hannah hid her cards well. It made him wonder. Would she ever open herself enough to trust him?

They'd never shared personal details in their chats. He'd told her the basics once, that he was a Harley-riding lawyer from California, but kept the full truth to himself. She hadn't wanted the details, and he hadn't wanted her to know them. He'd played a role, same as her. They had, however, spent long hours talking, about books, about life, sharing hopes, dreams, likes and dislikes. Even a few day-to-day frustrations. The kinds of things you shared with someone you were getting to know on an intimate level. Sharing things with someone he thought he'd never see came easily, especially with her.

It hadn't bothered him he didn't know her name, her family, her background. Until now. Until he sat watching her struggle with herself. Every once in a while, the façade would come down, and he'd catch a glimpse of the real Hannah, the woman. He had to admit, he yearned to know her softer side, yearned to learn what it would take to move beyond the walls she erected against him. The need scared the hell out of him.

Deep down, in a place he ought to wall back up, he yearned to see *her*, all of her, for the reprieve he suspected they'd both find in being themselves, and not what somebody wanted them to be. She *did* feel it, the pressure to be someone other than herself, or she wouldn't have lied about her looks. Someone had made her feel *less than*, and he hated it, because he knew what it was like not to meet someone's expectations.

Hannah dropped her gaze to his chest. A soft pink flush suffused her cheeks, and she hitched a shoulder in a halfhearted fashion. "You're it. You're the only man I'm seeing right now, and you have been for a while. Maybe that's pathetic, but it's the truth."

Ah, there it was, the soft heart she couldn't hide. Or perhaps she let down a wall or two. He had to admit her words made him want to shout from the rooftops again. For these two weeks, she was his.

She'd made the demand, but he had to admit it had merit. He'd been somebody's plaything one time too many. It was ironic to make that sort of demand in an arrangement like theirs, but he needed it as much as she did. For two weeks, she'd be his to enjoy. He could have his fill of her and get her out of his system.

The little devil on his shoulder laughed at him. Then why did the thought of never seeing her again, of going back to what they'd been, have his stomach dropping into his toes?

Ignoring the feeling, he hooked a finger beneath her chin, forced her gaze back to his, and offered her a smile.

"It's not pathetic. It's human, and it puts us on level playing field. Neither am I. I'd even take a guess it's for the same reason. Like I said, I know what it feels like to be used, so I understand why you asked. For the record, though, I have no desire to be with anybody else right now. I just want you." He released her chin and flashed a smile he didn't feel. He liked her, more than a little, and it scared the hell out of him. "I don't know about you, but I'm starved. How about we get dried off, and I'll put in a call to room service?"

He didn't wait for her answer but set her off his lap and rose from the tub.

* * *

Hannah stared as Cade exited the bath, grabbed an oversized fluffy towel from the metal rack, and held it open for her. His sudden change in mood hadn't escaped her notice. Their conversation had gone down a heavy road, because she'd gone and done what she shouldn't have—she'd voiced an insecurity. The walls had started coming down between them. She hadn't expected sex with him to be this intense. The man perplexed her. The playfulness they'd developed in their chats had followed them into their real exchanges, and being with him came as naturally as the beating of her heart.

His touch on her skin soothed as much as the rain pattering the windows lining the bathroom wall. They moved together, their bodies in sync, like they'd done it a thousand times. He didn't feel like a stranger at all, but a longtime lover her body knew on instinct. She hadn't expected that. How was it possible with a man she barely knew?

Except she did know him, deep down where it counted. She knew he liked to read erotica but preferred Stephen King. Knew he liked his coffee with cream *and* sugar, light bondage turned him on, and at the end of the day he preferred to relax with either a good book or the news, sometimes both. Cats made him sneeze and work took up ninety percent of his day.

She *needed* to set their relationship—however they chose to define it—back on track. Put a cap on it so it wouldn't get away from her. A man like him wouldn't have any use for a woman like her. They were from two different worlds, and if she allowed herself to get too involved, she'd find herself in love with a man who'd toss her aside like yesterday's underwear.

She had to admit, though, she wanted more than one night with him. Okay, so she didn't date much, but no man had ever looked at her or touched her the way he did. He made her feel beautiful. She could become addicted to that. She drew the line at two weeks, though. Any more time with him, and she had a feeling a broken heart lay in her future.

She turned and let him wrap the towel around her, using the position to her advantage. She didn't know if she wanted to see his expression when she said the words. "No strings. No dates. No emotions. So nobody gets hurt. Just sex."

He held her for a moment, hands resting on her shoulders. "Agreed."

Despite his agreement, unease hung between them, heavy and tangible. Their rules provided a harsh reality to something as intimate as sharing your body with someone. Online, she could turn her computer off and pretend she liked her single life, pretend lying in bed alone after sharing something so intimate with someone didn't feel wrong. Pretend it didn't hurt that he wasn't there with her.

And so it did then as well. Cade released her and yanked the second towel from the rack, wrapping it around his lean hips, then strode from the room without a backward glance. He obviously needed a bit of space to gather himself, so she took her time drying herself off and finger-combing her hair. Her makeup had drooped a bit, but she had to admit, her skin had a glow it hadn't had in a while.

She hung the towel back up and donned one of the robes on the back of the bathroom door, then joined Cade in the bedroom. He sat on the side of the bed, beside the nightstand. She froze in the doorway, feeling like a stranger again, stomach tied in knots, and he looked up as she entered. For a moment, neither said anything. They'd become caught somewhere between strangers and lovers. The unease reminded her of the awkward way she and Dane had related to each other a few months before he admitted to seeing someone else. She hated she had the same feeling with Cade, too.

"I didn't know what you liked, so I ordered a little bit of everything. We won't have to go out for a while." He smiled, warmth in his eyes.

Hannah's stomach did a little flip, a million giddy butterflies taking flight. Oh, Cade McKenzie had most definitely wooed a lot of ladies with that smile.

He held his hand out, and the power of his gaze pulled her to him. She went without question, crossing the room and slipping her hand into his. He used the purchase to pull her onto his lap, then wrapped both arms around her. "Nervous?"

Settled against his chest, he didn't feel so much like a stranger anymore. She shrugged. "A little."

"Me too. We'll get used to each other." He kissed her, gentle and languid, as if it were the first time all over again. Her stomach dipped and swayed with the nervous tension still fluttering inside of her. Tension continued to sit like a wall between them.

Cade cupped her head in the warmth of his large palms and tipped her, deepening the kiss. Hannah lost herself in the softness of his lips, in the gentle restless play of his tongue in her mouth. His kisses melted her defenses, and she couldn't stop herself from leaning into him. Beneath the thick robe, her nipples tightened, aching for the brush of his skin against her.

A quiet moan rumbled out of him. His cock hardened beneath her, digging into her bottom. Despite her recent orgasm, she grew moist all over again, her pussy clenching in anticipation.

She ached, more than she could ever remember, to feel him inside her again, pumping into her.

Cade turned her in his lap, laid her back on the bed, and stretched out beside her. One muscled thigh wedged between hers. He undid the sash of the robe, pulled open first one side, then the other, leaving her bare to his gaze once again.

She wanted to hide. He now had full view of the scars dotting her torso. The large one in her abdomen where the doctors had to stop internal bleeding. The others where shrapnel from the twisted metal and broken glass had cut into her skin, leaving small but permanent scars.

"The accident?" His voice came low and distracted as he followed the marks with his fingertips.

Hannah turned her head, stared at the white wall opposite, and nodded. She couldn't bring herself to say anything. She didn't want to know what he thought, couldn't bear if revulsion filled his eyes.

When his hot tongue traced the long, thick scar on her abdomen, she almost jumped out of her skin. She looked down in surprise to find him bent over her belly, grinning at her. He shifted, sliding over the top of her, and settled between her thighs, holding himself on his elbows. He kissed her once, then moved down her body inch by inch. His soft lips skimmed her jaw, down her throat and to her chest.

He moved from tiny scar to tiny scar. Gaze locked on her, he kissed each one, wickedness flashing in his eyes as he traced each one with the tip of his hot tongue. Every touch made her gasp, ramped up her desire to a level that left her squirming on the bed. Nobody had ever made her scars something arousing rather than shameful.

By the time he made his way back to her breasts again, her breaths came in short raspy pants, her embarrassment forgotten in the wash of hunger flooding her. Not giving her time to recover or form a coherent thought, one large, warm palm slid over the curve of each breast, cupping and massaging them.

"You're a perfect handful. Full and round. So beautiful." He let out an appreciative murmur, bending to swirl his tongue around each one.

Hannah gasped, a shiver running through her. He rolled the elongated tips between thumb and forefinger, then sucked on each one, and an outright needy cry erupted out of her. Her back arched off the bed, her breasts pushing themselves into his hands. She'd always had sensitive nipples, and his soft strokes and pinches made her crazy.

One hand left her breast, skimmed down her belly and over the inside of her right thigh. Her body stiffened as she waited for his touch to venture farther, for him to touch her where she needed him to.

"I've thought of touching you for months. I want to enjoy every inch of you while I have you, and I'm going to start by tasting you." He moved over the top of her, flicked his tongue along her lower lip, and kissed his way down her body again. All the while his hands stroked here and there, his touch so light he left goose bumps. By the time he settled between her thighs, she shivered and panted. Her body stiffened, waiting on the edge of a precipice for him to make the first, luscious stroke.

Tipping his head to look at her, he nudged her thighs apart, then leaned in and inhaled. His breath whispered over her sensitive flesh, and a quiet moan slid out of her. When he leaned in to taste her, a teasing little flick of his tongue along her slit, she shuddered.

He seemed to ignore her agony, or maybe he enjoyed it, for instead of diving in, his thumbs caressed her outer lips, soft and light, once, twice, before opening her. His hot breath whispered across her flesh. His tongue flicked out, grazing her swollen clit, the touch so light a helpless gasp left her. Every inch of her, every nerve ending, came alive, as if a livewire ran through her system. Every touch made her shudder, with an aching so keen she wanted to weep. He set a blaze inside of her.

She grabbed fistfuls of the comforter beneath her and squeezed her eyes shut. "Oh God. Cade, please."

"Please what, baby?" He pressed his mouth to her, scraping his teeth over the top of her mound, then blew a light stream of air over her exposed flesh. "Tell me what you want, Hannah."

The contrasting sensations, the cool air against her hot, wet folds, along with his teasing touches and the light flicks of his tongue, skirting away, never quite making contact, became too much to bear. Her hips bucked off the bed in desperate search of the contact she needed like she needed to draw her next breath. "Please!"

A deep rumble of laughter drifted from between her thighs. "Am I driving you crazy?"

Damn the man. He enjoyed tormenting her, the same way she had him earlier. She reached down, slid her hands into his hair. "Yes. Oh God, I'm at your mercy. Please, I need this."

"All right, baby. I'll put you out of your misery." He dipped his tongue inside, lapping at her inner folds in one long stroke.

Hannah thought for sure she'd explode right there. Oh, he was good at this. A desperate, needy moan slid out of her, her hips already rocking to the rhythm. "Oh, God, yes."

Cade moaned with her. "You taste good, baby. I always knew you'd taste sweeter than a summer peach."

"*Ohhhh.*" His hot words pushed her to the edge. A shudder of heat swept through her, deep and intense. "Cade…"

When he stroked her clit again, flicking back and forth with the lightness of a butterfly's wings, her fingers curled, fisting in his hair. He had her riding a fine, sweet edge. Every muscle in her body tensed, her clit so swollen, so sensitive she'd shatter at the slightest touch.

When he sucked the swollen nub into his mouth, a long, desperate moan ripped out of her. Her hips rocked forward. She let out a litany of muttered pleas, holding him to her and riding the press of his mouth, desperate to quench the fire. "Oh God, oh God, oh God."

Cade let out an outright growl this time. "Jesus, I can't stand it."

Any and all sense of teasing fled. He cupped her butt in his hands, lifting and angling her, and buried his face in her heat. His enthusiasm might have awed her had she not be so damn grateful. He sucked and licked at her swollen clit with wild abandon and like a flash of lightning, her orgasm struck, jolting and intense. Her body went taut, her legs stiffening. Hannah screamed. Her hips bucked against his mouth.

Cade held her firm against him and rode the wave with her all the way, his tireless tongue never once stopping, until she went limp, collapsing back into the bed, exhausted and spent. He kissed the inside of one thigh, then moved up beside her and pressed a tender kiss to her lips.

His breaths blew as harsh and ragged as hers, and his lips tasted of her. "You're delicious, baby. Getting to watch you come…God you're incredible."

She slid her hand up his thigh, palmed his cock, and stroked him once, then again. He moaned low in his throat, full of need, his hips rocking into her hand. Grateful for the gift he'd given her, she sat up, pushed him back and slid over top of him. It was his turn now. Hands braced on his chest, she straddled his hips. His cock lay hard and heavy against his stomach, caught between her slippery folds. With a roll of her hips, she slid along his length, riding him back and forth. Super sensitive post-orgasm, every soft stroke jolted through her, building her need all over again.

He leaned over, fishing a condom out of the nightstand drawer where he must have stashed them earlier and handed one to her. She slid down his body, rolled it on, and straddled him again. She wanted to take her time, to enjoy him, but she needed him too much. She lifted up but couldn't resist teasing and held herself there, poised over him.

His hands slid up her thighs, his fingers digging into her skin. "Don't tease."

Where she'd begged, Cade, clearly a dominating alpha male used to getting his way, demanded.

"As you wish, Master." Hannah smiled. She hoped he'd recognize the tease from their chats and sank down, taking him in one hard thrust. She aimed to give them what they both ached for, but she wanted him to see stars. He was easily the best lover she'd ever had, and she longed to give him what he'd given her.

"Holy mother of God." The words left his mouth barely a murmur. His eyes rolled back in his head before closing altogether. His hands moved to her hips. "You're like hot velvet, baby, so damn tight and slippery."

She lifted up until only the tip remained inside, then sank down hard again. His whole body quivered. His jaw clenched, the muscle jumping. Hannah did it again, rising and sinking hard. The ruthless rhythm pushed her past her limits. His thick cock hit every sensitive spot inside. Every thrust sent her reeling. Her thighs quivered as she teetered on the edge with him, her breaths coming hard and fast.

His fingers curled into her hips, digging into her skin. "Baby, you're killing me. Faster. Please, *God*, I need to go you faster."

His pleas filled her with a sense of freedom and power. Unable to resist, she grinned, rose up and sank again. This time, his hands clamped down on her, holding her firm. He began a punishing rhythm, hammering up into her again and again. The sounds of their heavy breathing, their bodies straining together, filled the room around them. Every time he filled her, he jarred the sweet place inside, sending a shower of hot sparks blazing through her with every flick of his hips. Her smile fell. She braced her hands on his chest and gave herself over to him.

Her climax struck out of nowhere, hot and blinding. Hannah cried out, her hips bucking against him of their own accord, riding the wave as it washed over her and sucked her under. Beneath her, he let out a long, agonized groan, his hips jerking as he found his own release.

She collapsed on his chest, her breathing harsh and erratic, and buried her face in his neck. His familiar, sexy scent filled her nostrils with every ragged breath. He wrapped his arms around her back, crushing her to him.

Then and there, the decision made itself. One night would never be enough to get him out of her system. It would be breaking a rule, but she needed this time with him. Her body responded to his in a way that rocked her world. She enjoyed him, all of him. She deserved to let herself have this time with him? Didn't she?

"Two weeks." She murmured the words into his throat, unable to bear releasing her hold on him even enough to meet his gaze. "No more, no less. When it ends, you go home and this doesn't happen again. No more phone calls. We go back to what we were."

She wanted sex, a fling with someone real and solid, but neither was she ready for more. Heck, hadn't he told her that very thing? And if she allowed this to continue, she'd no doubt become attached. She always did. No, it was safer for everybody involved if this was a one-time experience.

Cade went silent for a moment; then his arms tightened around her. "Agreed."

* * *

Several hours later, dressed once again in what she'd arrived in, Hannah tiptoed across the darkened bedroom. She paused in the doorway, one hand on the frame, unable to resist looking back. The digital alarm clock on the nightstand read 2:01. The bright moonlight streamed in through the windows lining one wall, illuminating the space. Cade lay on his back in the bed, naked, the sheets and blankets covering him from the waist down.

She couldn't help a soft, wistful smile. He looked peaceful. She'd woken because of the strangeness of his body beside her. She'd slept alone for so long that his physical presence beside her seemed odd in the otherwise routine of her life.

She left, however, because she liked it. Too much. She ached to crawl back up on the bed and curl around him. His body was large and solid and warm, and lying beside him filled her with an addictive sense of safety and rightness.

They'd made love off and on for hours, pausing to eat and chat or fulfill basic needs. Only to make love some more. His passion roused hers and over the course of a few hours, the uneasy tension they'd started with had dissolved. The comfort they'd found in their online chats opened between them here as well. Talking to him still came as natural as drawing her next breath. She'd forgotten her scars, and for a few blissful hours, he'd made her feel sexy and wanted.

Which was exactly why she was leaving.

She turned back around, moved through the room, and picked up her sandals off the floor where she'd dropped them in the living room. She made sure to close the door behind her as quietly as possible, so as not to disturb him. The silent hallway beyond unnerved her. She hadn't expected their exchanges to feel this natural. So she forced herself to leave, as she said she would. She'd have to be careful with him and make certain to draw her boundary lines. No matter how good or right being with him felt, this was only sex.

Right?

Chapter Five

Well, good for you." Several feet down the counter from her, Maddie stuck her leg out, nudging the toe of Hannah's sneaker. "It's about time you peeked outside the box you keep yourself in."

"I know, but can you blame me?" Hannah kept her gaze on her book. She had no desire to know what played on her best friend's face.

She sat on a stool, a few feet down the counter from where Maddie stood beside the register. The morning had been slow. As usual for early spring in Seattle, dark clouds blanketed the sky, a light rain misting the earth. With such a dreary day, people had kept indoors, and the call of the books around her had become too much to resist. She ought to be doing something more constructive. Perhaps if she'd decided to sort and shelve the new box of used books a woman had donated today, she might have avoided this exact conversation with Maddie.

Maddie, God bless her BFF, had cornered her first thing when she'd come into the shop this morning and pelted her with questions. She played devil's advocate. Any other time, Hannah appreciated Maddie playing the role. Her best friend was a "take no prisoners" kind of person, brave and up front. Where Hannah tended to be shy, Maddie often gave her the kick in the pants she needed. Now, however, it filled her mind with memories she didn't want to think about. Namely, her "date" with Cade the night before.

Ironically, the book she'd picked up was the second in the erotic series that had drawn her and Cade together in the first place. When the shop first opened, they'd dedicated the place to rare, out-of-print, or hard-to-find used books. The website also brought in a lot of traffic, people looking for specific titles. Last year, however, she and Maddie gave up the fight and decided to start carrying some of the new books coming out. More than a few people had requested this exact series. She'd made a killing off of it by advertising it in the front window. Sex sold. And well.

Maddie turned back to the stack of posters laid out on the counter in front of her. "Dane was a selfish jerk. You're better off without a man who doesn't have the balls to end one relationship before starting another. Those guys in college were asshats as well. Boys, the lot of 'em. What you need is a man, sweetie. I've told you that." Maddie plucked the largest poster from the pile and strode around the counter, heading toward the front window display. "So, is he? I take it the scars didn't bother him if you spent the night with him."

Hannah's gaze paused halfway down the page as the memory filled her mind. The fifteen minutes or so Cade had spent paying homage to each of her scars flashed through her mind.

Her panties dampened, and a luscious throb began. Hannah squirmed on her stool.

Embarrassed warmth rushed up her neck and into her cheeks. The exact reason she tried not to think about him. The mere thought of him had her looking forward to the next time she'd see him. The way she reacted to him was dangerous at best. He made her heart beat a little faster and anticipation fizzled through her blood like a new drug she couldn't get enough of.

Maddie glanced back over her shoulder and grinned, her bright red braid falling back off her shoulder. Her best friend had Irish ancestors. Her grandfather, the man who'd raised her, had come over somewhere after World War I. Maddie had the classic look—pale, almost porcelain skin, dotted generously with freckles, gorgeous deep-red hair, and pale blue eyes. Her luxurious mane had always made Hannah jealous. It was thick and soft and even fresh out of bed, she always seemed to look stylishly tousled. Today, it hung in a neat brain down her back, and those shrewd eyes pinned Hannah with a mischievous glint.

"I'll take that as a no." Maddie set the poster on the windowsill and moved back toward the counter, reaching for the tape. "I think it was a good move to give in and order these books. They've…"

The front door's digital chime beeped, announcing the entrance of a customer, and Maddie's words trailed off into nothing. Her best friend's sudden cease in conversation told Hannah without a doubt someone of the male persuasion had walked through the door.

Maddie confirmed the thought when she kicked Hannah's

shoe again, her voice a hoarse whisper in the space between them. "Dibs."

Hannah smiled but didn't look up. Nothing turned Maddie on more than a guy who read. If he had good looks on top of it, the poor guy didn't stand a chance. Which meant any halfway decent-looking guy who happened upon their little eclectic store got the once-over and a smile to charm the pants off the pope.

She and Maddie had chosen this particular spot for their shop on purpose. They sat almost dead center of the downtown street, a few blocks from Pike Place Market. Next door was a small bakery. The man who owned it had earned a spot on a local television show for "the best chocolate chip cookies on the West Coast." Two doors down sat a chocolate shop. The woman had garnered a reputation for making the most divine handmade chocolates. Which put their store in a prime location. Tourists often wandered in off the street in their tour of the city.

Like her, Maddie didn't date. She'd met too many of the wrong kinds of men. It was what had drawn them together in the first place. She'd been lamenting Dane's constant lack of attention. Unlike her, Maddie had taken a firm vow of celibacy. Deep down, her best friend was a hopeless romantic and a shameless flirt. Maddie, of course, hoped Prince Charming would one day waltz in and sweep her off her feet.

"Good morning! Welcome to Second Chance Books." Maddie shot around the counter like a bee on too much caffeine.

Hannah didn't need to look to know her best friend's smile would put the sun to shame. Maddie's enthusiastic tone said it all.

Hannah lifted her gaze, curious to see the poor unlucky soul who'd happened upon their little store, only to freeze on her stool. Her heart leapt into her throat and beat like a jackhammer. Oh God. Cade. In a full business suit no less. A crisp, white shirt and charcoal-gray slacks topped by a jacket in the same shade of gray, complete with a little splash of blue peeking out the pocket on his left breast.

The sight of him in all his splendor did nothing for the dry state of her panties. She'd never seen him in a suit before, had always pictured him in jeans and a leather jacket, but she had to admit, he looked spectacular. The suit hugged his body in all the right places, accentuating his broad shoulders and long, muscular legs. He looked sophisticated and intelligent, completely contradicting his biker-boy persona online.

His head turned left and right, his gaze taking in his surroundings as he strolled, casually, into the store. As if he were a tourist who'd happened to find them on his way through downtown. "Nice place. Quaint. It suits you."

Hannah swallowed past the lump stuck in her throat and sat up, closing the book and setting it on the counter in front of her. She ran a shaky hand through her hair. Thank God she always put on makeup in the morning. "W-what are you doing here?"

He fingered the edge of the display Maddie had set by the front windows, then turned to the hardback books seated in their place and flipped open the cover, those shrewd eyes scanning the page.

"You invited me to look you up, so I did. Turns out, you weren't hard to find, either. When you said you were downtown, I didn't realize you'd end up being so close." He turned his head, finally meeting her gaze, and crossed the space between them in three long strides. He leaned in front of her, his gaze on the book lying on the counter. He tapped the cover before glancing at her. Wolfish delight glittered like diamonds in his eyes. "I haven't read this one yet. Is it any good?"

The heat in his eyes filled her mind with memories of their initial encounters, of the e-mails and chat messages shot back and forth over that first book. *Have you ever been spanked during sex? You should try it before you decide you don't like it.* The heated conversations his questions had led them to made her clit throb all over again.

She swallowed hard and repeated her question. "What are you doing here?"

He turned his hand over on the counter, palm up, and stared at her. "I thought you might like to have lunch with me."

His scent invaded her nostrils every time she inhaled. Alarm skittered up her spine, and her hands trembled, out of physical need and nerves. After the intimacy they'd shared the day before, she hoped to put some distance between them, reset those boundary lines. He'd changed the rules—again—and it set her off balance. Damn him.

It worked. The gleam in his eye and his suggestive tone had every inch of her sitting up and taking notice. She yearned to lean across the counter and wipe the smug smile off his face by pushing her mouth into his.

She averted her gaze instead and moved down the counter to the pile of paperwork near the register, pretending to busy herself. "We agreed no dates."

"This isn't a date. It's lunch. We both have to eat, and I'm starved."

Darting a glance out of the corner of her eye, she found him watching her. The gleam in his eyes, the subtle flash of heat, sent a shiver of the same down her spine. She wanted to send him back out of the shop, but her thighs clenched, her clit throbbing to life and begging for the stroke of his oh-so-talented tongue. It didn't help she had the distinct impression he didn't mean food.

Somewhere off to her left, Maddie cleared her throat.

Hannah swallowed hard, heat flooding her cheeks. Oh God. She'd gotten so caught up in him she'd forgotten Maddie entirely. That wasn't a good sign.

She turned to flash her best friend a sheepish grin, only to get a saucy one in return.

Hannah turned to Cade, extending a hand toward Maddie. "My business partner and best friend, Madison O'Riley. Maddie, this is—"

"Cade McKenzie." He pushed away from the counter and extended a hand, offering a charming smile. "Mind if I borrow your cohort for an hour or so?"

Maddie slipped her hand into his, shaking it firmly, and flashed him a thousand-watt smile.

"Oh no. Please. Borrow her for as long as you like." Maddie winked at him. "She could use a break."

The heat in Hannah's cheeks deepened. Maddie's sassy little wink told her without a doubt she'd caught the hint in Cade's tone as well.

"I appreciate it, thanks." Cade turned back to Hannah, took the papers from her and set them on the counter, then held out his hand. "It's only lunch."

Hannah stared at his hand, because if she met his gaze, she'd give in. Obviously, Cade McKenzie didn't take no for an answer.

A million thoughts shot through her mind, things she ought to say to him. He'd changed the rules, damn it, and he hadn't discussed the change with her. She would not be a pawn in somebody else's game.

Except the memory of the ecstasy she'd had at the mercy of those large, soft hands and his wicked mouth wouldn't leave her thoughts. Her hand slipped itself into his, and a flood of warmth infused her every cell.

He threaded their fingers, waited as she grabbed her purse, then held their combined hands over their heads as she rounded the counter. He turned to smile at Maddie. "I'll have her back in an hour. Scout's honor."

He made a gesture with his fingers, making her wonder if he really had been a Boy Scout, then pulled open the door and tugged her outside with him. Maddie flashed a too-pleased grin as they stepped onto the sidewalk and the door dinged shut.

A heady buzz followed them down the street and anticipation fizzled in her veins. When they reached the end of the block and stopped to wait for the light, she glanced at him. "Are we really going to lunch?"

He turned his head and cocked a brow. "Do you trust me?"

She let out a nervous laugh and shook her head. "I don't know you well enough to trust you."

His smile fell. The light turned, but he pivoted to her instead and took both her hands in his. He used the purchase to pull her close and leaned down, brushing his mouth over hers. "You know me better than you think you do. How much of what you told me during our chats was a façade?"

Caught in the brush of his body against hers and his warm

breath on her face, Hannah couldn't remember if she breathed. "Not much."

Cade was easy to talk to and always had been. The lure of the anonymity of the Internet had pulled things from her she might not have told him otherwise.

"Exactly." He brushed his mouth over hers again, so light and electric a shiver ran the length of her spine. Her hands curled in his, and she leaned into the soft press of his lips.

Cade flicked his tongue against her mouth and leaned his head beside her ear. He murmured against the sensitive lobe, his breath hot on her neck.

"I know we didn't agree on this, but I made plans for you. I'm hoping you'll enjoy them as much I will. I'm asking you to trust me." When he pulled back again, heat flashed in his eyes. "I had to see you."

His kiss made her knees wobble and promised more where that came from. His hot gaze did the same. His erection pushed into her stomach, promising orgasms lay in her future. It would no doubt get her into trouble one day soon, but Cade McKenzie had her eating out of the palm of his hand. She'd follow him anywhere for the pleasure that instinct said she'd have at his hands.

God help her.

Hannah nodded. "All right."

He pressed another kiss to her lips, this one a hot promise.

"You won't be sorry." He released her and stepped back, holding her away from him. His gaze flicked down her body. "Though I do wish you were wearing a skirt."

* * *

Fifteen minutes later, Cade sat across from Hannah in a small booth at a pub down the street. She looked gorgeous. Her black and white striped blouse skimmed her body, and her dark-washed jeans hugged every luscious curve. She sat on the other side of the booth and not beside him because he flat out didn't trust himself not to touch her. He hadn't been able to stop thinking about her all damn morning. Lunch was little more than an excuse to see her.

He'd chosen this place on purpose. A client had recommended it a few days prior as a good place to grab lunch. It had a dark, intimate, old pub look about it, and the place had gathered a decent crowd. Surely they wouldn't be missed if they disappeared for, oh, say, five minutes.

He picked up his phone from the table, punched in the text he'd planned earlier, and hit SEND. Then he waited. Across the booth, a muted buzz came from the vicinity of the bench seat beside Hannah. In the process of studying the menu laid out on the table in front of her, she lifted her gaze, the question in her eyes.

He set his phone on the table and sat back. "Answer it."

Watching her dig her phone out of her small clutch and read the text exerted more patience than he had. He'd been hard all morning. The thought alone made him want to laugh. He'd always prided himself on being professional. The job always came first. He'd earned his position through hard work and dedication, often to the point of ignoring basic needs. These days, work provided a much-needed escape from the mess Amelia had entangled him in and the hurt and mistrust she'd left behind. He hadn't intended to date again anytime soon.

Since he'd met Hannah six months ago, he spent a good majority of his day with a hard-on. Thank God for long suit jackets. Luckily, he'd spent this morning in meetings, seated behind a boardroom table going through paperwork and last-minute details.

Hannah looked up from her phone, eyes wide with alarm. "Here?"

The disbelief written in her tone made him want to laugh. His head hadn't been in the game this morning because of her. The problem had started when he woke without her. Waking alone ought to feel natural. After all, he did it every morning. Not to mention they'd agreed her staying would complicate their arrangement.

Except he'd hated waking alone. Her softness beside him in bed last night had been a lure he missed when he woke without her. It nudged the loneliness in his gut, a feeling he needed to ignore. He loathed the monotony of his life. His entire world revolved around contract negotiations and legal documents and dating women who'd be assets to his family's good name. Waking alone every morning had grown tiresome. He longed for one woman who'd see *him*, who'd fill the empty space within.

When a two-hour window opened for lunch this afternoon, he found himself researching Hannah online. Turned out, her bookstore sat a few blocks from where his business took place. Halfway here, he passed the same streets they'd walked when they left the Space Needle the day before. Their conversation that day had filled his thoughts and an idea had grabbed him he hadn't been able to resist.

Of course, this little lunch escapade meant he'd begun to dream up excuses to see her.

"Here." He nodded and looked down at his phone, typing in another message.

CMcKenzie: Are you afraid?

Okay, call him a rebel. He spelled out his texts. He loathed shorthand. He understood the need, but he refused to use it. It made the sender look unintelligent. He'd rather take his time.

He hit SEND, then lifted his gaze, arching a brow in challenge.

Hannah looked up from her phone and darted an anxious glance around, then sat straighter in her seat. "No. Just nervous."

This time, a becoming soft pink suffused her cheeks. Her fingers trembled as she typed a return message.

Hannah: We'll get caught

Cade suppressed a smile as he punched in a quick reply.

CMcKenzie: That's the thrill, baby. You have no idea how hard I am. Bathroom. I'll order, then follow.

Hannah hesitated, staring at her screen. He pushed her limits, but the thought of her hot gaze locked on his, eyes hooded with desire as she watched him in the mirror would be the ultimate payoff. He typed in another message.

CMcKenzie: Do you want me?

Heat flashed in her eyes, answering the question, but her fingers flew over her phone's tiny keyboard.

Hannah: Badly

Cade stifled a groan as he punched in another message.

CMcKenzie: And does the thought of me fucking you here arouse you?

He sat back in the bench seat and arched a brow. "Tell me the truth."

The pink in her cheeks deepened. She didn't answer but dropped her gaze to her lap.

Hannah: I'm so wet and my clit is throbbing.

He growled. She had a sexual appetite that burned him from the inside out. The thought of her sitting over there, hot and wet, had his cock thickening behind his fly. His hands had begun to shake with need.

He narrowed his eyes at her. "Go. I'll order."

Five minutes later, he waited in the hallway outside the women's bathroom. Standing there, unease sifted through him. He had to admit he hadn't thought this out well. Fucking her in the bathroom was high school kid stuff, not to mention risky. Christ, if he ended up in the paper for this, his father would flip. His father had an image he wanted to uphold and strict rules all the lawyers in his firm were expected to follow, him included.

He had no idea how they'd even carry it out. People packed the place. Four people had passed him in the minutes he spent waiting in the hallway. An older gentleman exiting the men's bathroom didn't as much as glance in his direction. A woman in a business suit exited the woman's restroom next, however, and came up short at finding him waiting outside.

Heart pounding in this throat, he flashed a polite smile and folded his arms. "Waiting for my wife."

Her mouth opened in a silent "ah" and she nodded in return, moving around him down the hallway. When she disappeared into the dining area, he rapped twice on the woman's restroom door. Two seconds later, it opened, and Hannah poked out her head. She grabbed his arm and pulled him inside. The door barely closed behind him before she was pressing him back against it.

She molded her mouth to his and reached behind him to turn the lock. She was panting, her mouth hard on his, her tongue restless in his mouth. Her hands trembled as she reached for his fly, fumbling with his belt buckle.

"I thought for sure someone would say something to me out there." He reached for the button on her jeans in turn, popping it free. "We'll have to be fast."

Hannah murmured against his mouth, something incoherent he didn't catch as she unzipped his slacks. In seconds she had his cock in her hand, stroking him in her warm palm, and whatever doubt he had was lost in the luscious stroke of her expert fingers and soft skin.

He swore under his breath and shackled her wrist. If she kept it up, the fireworks would come a lot sooner than he hoped. Right then, he needed to watch her come undone. He'd dreamed up this whole scenario for her. He'd become addicted to knowing he could undo her the way she did him.

"Mirror." He turned her, steering her to the sink. The mirror filled the entire wall, tall and wide enough he could see everything. Her breasts heaved beneath her blouse, her nipples hard and poking against the fabric. She turned to the sink, shoved her jeans and panties down, widened her stance as much as possible, and wiggled her ass in impatience.

Desperate to know, he slid a hand down her round bottom and between her thighs. She moaned, pushing back into him. His fingers slipped in with ease, and her juices coated his hand. Christ. She really was aroused by this.

Shaking now, he shoved his pants to his knees. His trembling fingers fumbled over the condom, so that it took him two tries to get the damn thing on. With a needy groan, he grabbed her hips and pushed into her in one quick thrust. She let out a soft moan, her body already trembling in his arms, and met his gaze in the mirror. The heat in her eyes seared him from the inside out.

He leaned to his right, waved a hand beneath the automatic dryer for noise to stifle their moans, and leaned over her back. He nibbled her shoulder, her neck, her jaw, any part of her he could reach. God, his need for her…

"You'll have to forgive me, baby. I don't have it in me for finesse or tenderness right now. I need you. Badly. I have since I got up this morning. Jesus, Hannah, I'm so fucking hard. I want to watch you fall apart in my arms, feel your pussy clamping around my cock…"

She moaned. Biting her lip, she didn't ask for any softness, either. Rather, she gave as good as she got. Her hips pushed into his, soft little purrs emanating from her throat. She reached back, sliding her hand over his hip to his ass, and pulled him harder against her. He increased his tempo, lost in the moment, in her. The sound of their need for each other filled his ears, fueling his own. Their bodies coming together hard. Their harsh breathing.

In what had to be record time, Hannah tossed her head back, her eyes closing. A mix between torment and bliss crossed her features. Her fingers curled into his ass, nails biting into his skin as she let out a soft moan. "Cade…I'm…*Oh God*…"

No sooner had the whispered words left her mouth than she shuddered in his arms, her convulsing body pulling his orgasm from him at blinding speed. Cade clamped his mouth on her shoulder to stifle the moan ripping from his chest.

By the time their orgasms subsided, both were left shaking and panting. Her body went limp. He didn't know if he could move let alone stand upright.

"You are fucking incredible." He hooked her chin with a finger and turned her head enough to brush a kiss across her mouth, then forced himself to straighten. They wouldn't have long before someone noticed the door was locked.

Hannah drew a breath between her teeth and moaned as he pulled out of her. They spent the next minute yanking up clothing. As he buckled his belt, someone pounded on the restroom door.

They both jumped. Cade cursed under his breath. Hannah's eyes widened, panic flashing across her face. Jesus. If they got caught, the place would throw them out and it would no doubt be all over the news. If he ended up on the five o'clock news, he could kiss his partnership goodbye.

Before he could make his brain work enough to think of what to do, Hannah grabbed him by the shoulders and shoved him into a stall, closing the door behind her. She peeked through the slit in the door, a finger held to her lips, then moved away. The sound of water running filled the room, then the metal grinding of a key in a lock, followed by the creak of the door opening.

"Oh. I'm sorry, ma'am. I didn't realize anyone was in here. Do you know why this door was locked?"

The unfamiliar male voice held distrust and suspicion. Heart hammering in his throat, Cade shifted in the stall, peeking through the slat where the door didn't quite meet the frame. Every inch of him tensed and regret churned in his gut. He'd never run from anything in his life. He was being a damn coward, hiding in a stall and letting Hannah take the fall for what had been his stupid idea.

He reached for the door handle when Hannah's gaze flicked to his. Her eyes widened, her jaw tightening, and she gave a barely there shake of her head. Then she pivoted and turned, moving out of his line of sight.

"You mean to tell me somebody locked me in here?" Hannah's voice rose in indignation. "Who the hell would lock someone in a bathroom?"

"I'm very sorry, ma'am. I have no idea. We were alerted by a customer who couldn't get inside."

The man sputtered an apology, and Cade wished like hell he could see. From the sound of things, Hannah put on the performance of a lifetime.

"Well, you should find out, because someone obviously did. If they want to lock the bathrooms, they should make sure nobody's in here first!"

"I'm very sorry, ma'am. I'll make sure I pass on the message. I assure you it won't happen again."

Cade shook his head. He felt sorry for the poor schmuck who'd found them. Hannah's attack had clearly surprised him so much it hadn't occurred to him the door locked from the inside.

"Thank you." An indignant *humph* sounded in the room; then the bathroom door opened with a squeak. Two seconds later, Hannah ripped the stall door open, eyes wide and round. "Oh my God, that was close. I'll go out first and knock on the wall when the coast is clear."

She turned and left before he'd even managed to utter a thank you. The rap on the wall came a few seconds later, and he exited the bathroom with his heart in his throat. Hannah waited for him in the hallway. He claimed her hand, threading their fingers, needing the solid presence of her to keep him from coming apart. He led her back to their table still shaking. His heart continued to hammer a panicky rhythm, throbbing in his ears.

When he slid into his side of the booth, he released his held breath and finally allowed himself to relax. Looking around, nobody even seemed to notice their absence. Their lunch had arrived, neatly waiting for them. Every table was full, the diners all engrossed in their lunches and conversations. Waiters and waitresses carried trays of food and drinks. Not a single person glanced in their direction.

Cade opened his mouth, to apologize, to thank her, to…something. Regret and gratitude had caught in his chest and needed to find its way out. Never in his life had he done something so risky. His father would have a coronary.

Across the table, an insane little giggle erupted from Hannah. She clamped a hand over her mouth and giggled again behind her fingers. "Oh my God. I can't believe we did that."

Her expression had his mind twisting off in another direction. Regret forgotten, the knot in his stomach eased. He must have a stupid grin on his face. Her eyes glowed from within, and she continued to laugh.

He sat back in the booth, triumph and awe swelling in his chest. She really was incredible. The risk of getting caught and ending up on the front page of the *Seattle Times* had been worth it to see the light in her eyes. "I take it you enjoyed yourself, Miss Miller?"

She dropped her hands away from her face. Heat flashed like a solar flare in the depths of her golden eyes. "I enjoyed the hell out of myself, as if you didn't know. I…"

She held up a finger and picked up her cell phone, her fingers flying over the keyboard. When she finished, she looked up and nodded in his direction.

Cade plucked his phone from the inside pocket of his suit jacket.

Hannah: To quote somebody I know, I think I saw stars I came so hard. We should do that again.

Cade glanced back up. Hannah grinned at him. She had a wide mouth and full lips and her bright smile became the focal point in her face. For a moment, he could only stare, stunned. Mission accomplished. They'd almost gotten caught, but she beamed at him.

God, he was in trouble. That look and the feeling eating up his insides meant one thing. Hannah Miller had gotten under his skin, but right then, he couldn't be sorry for it. The light in her eyes had captured him. She radiated like the sun. He'd make a fool out of himself to put that joy back in her eyes.

* * *

He dropped her off in front of her store a half hour later. The moment caught him in the chest. The intimacy they'd developed had become painfully apparent. They'd walked the few blocks back to her store in companionable silence, her hand warm and right in his.

He liked the man he became with her by his side. She relaxed him, so much so he'd gone to the lengths he had to set up their tryst this afternoon. Something he never did. Hannah pulled him out of his rigid routines and made him do things he'd never have contemplated otherwise, just to see her smile.

She made him forget himself, his name, the obligations he'd worked so damned hard for. This made two times he'd lost his head around her, but he could only be sorry for one thing.

He caught her around the waist, holding her close. "I owe you an apology."

Her brow furrowed. "What on earth for?"

He shook his head. "That didn't go as planned. I was a coward to hide in the stall while you handled that guy."

She stared at him for a moment, gaze working over his face.

"And what? Let you get caught so we can get kicked out of there? I haven't had that much excitement in a while. I enjoyed the hell out of that. You getting caught wouldn't have done anybody any good." She lifted onto her toes, hands braced on his chest, and caught his bottom lip between her teeth. Her voice lowered to a husky murmur. "Next time, I'll surprise you."

She winked, then turned and moved into the shop, the electronic beep sounding as the door floated closed behind her. As she approached Maddie behind the counter, his earlier thought cemented. How the hell it was possible to feel as close to someone as he did to her in two days, he didn't know, but Hannah Miller had become a part of him.

The problem was, he liked her there. He could easily get lost in everything about her that made her so damn addicting. The soft, guileless way she smiled at him. Her quiet, breathy laughter. With her, he had the sensation of being king of the world, like he could accomplish anything, so long as she kept smiling at him.

Being with her humbled him. She didn't judge him, but accepted him, faults and all. Even online, for a few precious hours, he had no name, no obligations, and no pressure to be top dog. He could be himself. He didn't have that particular luxury much, and he appreciated the hell out of it now. It made him long to confide in her, to share Ethan with her.

All of which meant he'd gone off the deep end. He needed to put some distance between them, make up an excuse to be busy tonight and concentrate on the business he'd come to Seattle for in the first place. The last pieces of the merger needed to be completed. He had enough paperwork to occupy his time. When the deal finished, he'd go home and this insanity with Hannah would end.

And it *would* end. She was only a warm body. Granted, a sweet, alluring body he craved and a mind he ached with every fiber of his being to know, but their relationship consisted of sex, no more, no less. He'd do well to remember that.

Chapter Six

Hannah closed her eyes with a sigh. The darkness of the bedroom and the quietness of the night provided a lull, but sleep wouldn't come. She'd hoped to see Cade tonight. He'd sent her a text two days before telling her he'd be busy for a few days, but otherwise, she hadn't seen hide nor hair of him since their afternoon tryst the other day. It shouldn't bother her. After all, she had no hold on him, save their agreement not to sleep with anyone else for these two weeks. She couldn't even call herself his girlfriend.

Yet no matter how hard she tried to ignore it, she couldn't stop the disappointment from surging through her. She'd been put off enough to know he was avoiding her. Standing with him in front of the store the other day, something intense blazed at the back of his eyes. The hamster wheel had been turning. She had a feeling the hamster was always running in his mind, because his eyes seemed to take in everything around him. Cade McKenzie was a watcher, like her. Something in the depths of his eyes had nagged at her.

She hadn't meant to invite herself to initiate their next tryst. She *ought* to be putting distance between them. Except their encounter in the bathroom had blown her mind. Being with Cade had become so easy and so addicting. In person, the chemistry between them intensified. Her body responded to his.

His impulsive idea had been naughty and exquisite. The risk of getting caught had been a thrill zinging through her veins, which only heightened the intensity. Getting to watch his lids droop and the heat and hunger rise in his eyes as he pounded into her from behind. The memory filled her head all over again and her insides clenched with need.

His regret afterward, though, had been palpable and it had rendered her defenseless. She'd been the one to talk their way out of getting caught and it clearly bothered him. Cade had always been an alpha, an in-control kind of man and obviously used to playing the role, but his concern melted her knees. It had been a long time since anyone wanted to stand up for her.

His chivalry made her yearn to melt into him, which meant she'd caught sight of his human side. She had no desire to see faults and human frailties. Those parts of him would only make her fall in love with him. Cade McKenzie was so far out of her league as to be humorous. They shared a fling, nothing more, nothing less, and something to be tossed aside when it ended.

Which was why she'd decided to stay home tonight instead of surprising him, as she'd said she would. He hadn't called her. She wouldn't go traipsing after him like a lovesick puppy.

The buzz of her phone as it vibrated on her nightstand jerked her out of her heavy musings. She turned her head, following the sound. The red numbers on her digital clock read 11:57 p.m. Despite every previous thought, her heart thumped in anticipation as she sat up, leaning on an elbow to grab her phone. A text blinked across her screen in neon green.

CMcKenzie: Hey, baby. Any chance you're still awake?

Her heart skipped a full giddy beat. His text meant one thing: he was awake at midnight thinking about her, too.

She sucked the corner of her lower lip into her mouth and bit down. She shouldn't want to talk to him tonight. He hadn't so much as called, and it bothered her. It meant he'd become too important. She'd started to do stupid things like hope, things that would get her heart broken again. She *needed* to start dating again, see other men so she'd stop pinning her heart's hopes on this one impossible dream. Cade was a billionaire's son, heir to more money than she could ever fathom. She was that child nobody wanted.

Except she'd promised him that for these two weeks, she'd be his and his alone. She liked the thought more than a little. She liked *Cade*. She enjoyed him. Being with him physically seemed a natural next step to their relationship.

Thoughts whirled in confusing circles in her mind. Her fingers brought up the text and punched in a reply before she could talk herself out of it.

Hannah: it's late.

His reply popped up seconds later. That fact did nothing for the giddy butterflies in her stomach.

CMcKenzie: Sorry. Did I wake you?

Should she tell him the truth?

Hannah: Would you feel bad if I said yes?

CMcKenzie: No. ;)

Hannah couldn't help her grin or the hitch to her heartbeat. He could be a cocky son of a bitch sometimes. She'd always found this aspect of him sexy.

Hannah: Well, then you're in luck. I was awake.

CMcKenzie: Can't sleep?

Her fingers paused over the keypad. *Don't do it. Don't tell him. Lie. Tell him you were reading.*

Once again, her fingers didn't obey.

Hannah: No. Didn't think I'd talk to you tonight.

Okay, so she'd been hoping. She couldn't resist the luscious pull of Cade's presence in the city. After all, she'd only have him for two weeks. Two weeks, then he'd go home, never to be seen again, back to being a name on her computer screen, if she ever heard from him again at all. She'd go back to the loneliness and emptiness her life had become. The thought of going through the dating process again brought a deep, abiding sense of dread. She didn't look forward to the stares, to the excuses, to the creeps who'd use her up and spit her out.

Her phone dinged, Cade's reply almost immediate. The thought did nothing for the tangle of emotion caught in her chest.

CMcKenzie: Sorry. Work's crazy. My days are booked solid and my nights are for preparing for the next day. Lots I need to get done.

Something akin to envy surged in her chest, but she squashed it. She couldn't stake a claim on him. They didn't belong to each other. *This is a fling. Remember?*

Time to steer this conversation back into safer territory.

Hannah: What is it you do, exactly, GQ?

CMcKenzie: Mergers & acquisitions. Right now, I'm working on a merger. Two large companies consolidating.

Hannah: Sounds exciting.

Okay, so it didn't. She attempted to stall him. He'd contacted her and her heart had glommed onto this small bit of him.

CMcKenzie: LOL. I'm afraid I'm bit of a nerd. It's a lot of late nights drafting documents & getting paperwork ready for filing. I enjoy things like reading & research. Always have.

Hannah: Nerds r sexy

She meant that. Sincerely. In all the wrong kinds of ways. Nerds were the guys you settled down with, because you could depend on them, and a dependable man could make her cream her panties.

CMcKenzie: Glad you think so. Most women I've come across don't appear to. What were you doing before I called?

Hannah gnawed on her lower lip. She shouldn't tell him the truth. No, she ought to make up an excuse and go back to sleep. He hadn't called in two days and it left her with the feeling of being somebody's beck-and-call girl. Something she'd been one time too many. Maybe she should have anticipated this. She couldn't expect the man to drop everything for her. After all, she meant nothing to him. They were lovers, nothing more.

Excerpt she couldn't deny she yearned to see him, if only to talk to him in the dark.

Hannah: Thinking about you & lunch the other day.

CMcKenzie: Funny. Me too. Want some company?

Hannah hesitated. Did she? Without a doubt. The thought of him coming over and being in her apartment rather than words on a screen made her wet all over again. *Should* she? This time, she had to be honest.

Hannah: 3 hours ago? Hands down. Now? It's late. I have to get up early.

CMcKenzie: Bummer. Guess I should've called first, then.

Called first? What on earth did he mean he should have called first? Halfway through typing out the question, the doorbell sounded through the apartment.

Her heart skipped a full beat this time. She threw the covers back and sprang from the bed, trying not to run to the door. She peered through the peephole. Cade stood out in the hallway, five o'clock shadow and all.

She undid the locks with shaking fingers and pulled the door open, too stunned for a moment to do much more than take in his tall, broad form leaning in her doorway. He had on his pajamas, too, baggy, blue plaid pants hanging low on his hips, a plain white T-shirt, and, of all things, running sneakers.

She darted an obvious glance down his body and raised her brows. "Last-minute decision?"

Phone in one hand, he hitched a shoulder, nonchalant. As if he showed up on women's doorsteps in his pajamas at midnight all the time. Something hot and promising flashed in his gaze, though, and her stomach dipped in the most exquisite way. "Something like that."

A sense of vulnerability washed through her chest, and her smile fell. She ached to jump on him, to wrap her body around him and drag him inside. She couldn't deny the sight of him filled her with joy to near bursting. "I didn't think I'd get to see you tonight."

"Me neither." He pushed away from the doorway and stepped over the threshold. "I hadn't intended to come over. Prepping for tomorrow took longer than I expected. It got late and I thought for sure you'd be sleeping. But I couldn't go to sleep without seeing you."

"Is that why you haven't called in two days?" She hadn't meant to ask him that, but the expression on his face and the tension mounting between them nagged at her. Something was off. She'd heard enough excuses over the years from guys backpedaling their way out of a date to know when someone was avoiding her. She'd rather Cade be honest with her.

He remained silent, his gaze searching hers. Great. She sounded like a jealous girlfriend.

Cade took another step, closing the door behind him and moving into her personal space. So close every time she inhaled, his scent invaded her nostrils.

"No. You're right. I've been avoiding calling you. You make me crazy, Hannah. I'm in meetings I need to be paying attention to and all I can think about is you. Almost getting caught the other day scared the hell out of me. You want the truth? I don't do crazy or impulsive. I do safe. I do what's expected of me, and I do it well, *because* it's expected of me."

He lifted a hand, stroking her cheek, awe in his gaze as it worked her face.

"But with you? I find myself dreaming up ways to rock your damn world. Like fucking you in a public place, because I know, deep down, it turns you on. I don't take risks like that, but I like making you happy. Getting to watch you is the most erotic thing I've ever seen, and your smile afterward was all the reward I needed."

He cupped her face in the warmth of his huge hands. Hannah was helpless to do anything but stare. His heartfelt words had hit their mark. Cade McKenzie was a good man, and she was melting beneath the power of him.

"So, no, I hadn't intended to come over tonight. I wanted some time to get my head together, but in the end, I couldn't stand it. I had to see you."

His words lodged themselves deep within. She understood only too well. She didn't want to. Instinct said she'd broken all those rules she used to live by once, and it insisted she shove him back out of her life. He'd become far too important, when, in the end, despite his words, the two weeks would end and he'd go back to his life. Without her. Except right here, in this moment, they connected on a deeper level. They gave each other something they both needed. She may not understand what it meant for him, she may not ever know, but she understood the basic need behind it.

She opened her mouth, but he didn't give her time to form a response. Instead, he bent his head, silencing her by covering her mouth with his. He crushed her to him, his tongue restless and searching. His body shook as hard as hers. God help her, she answered. Her tongue sought his in return. Her hands slid up his chest, pulling him as close as she could get him. The solid warmth of his hard pecs rubbing her nipples made her want to weep with the pleasure coursing through her. She wanted to wrap herself around him and never come out. The way she craved him made her knees shake.

He let out a quiet moan, a sound of agony and relief, and nipped at her bottom lip before sweeping her off her feet.

"Bedroom." The single word left his mouth on a hot demand. She didn't have it in her to deny him.

"Back of the apartment." She leaned her head in, nibbling her way up his neck. He smelled incredible. His cologne was a hint on his skin, mixing with the scent of clean male and bringing images of him in the bath the last time she'd been in his hotel room.

Halfway through the front room, her gaze landed on the couch. Her laptop sat in its usual spot on the coffee table. She jerked her head up. "Wait. The couch."

He shook his head as he carried her past. "Bed is bigger. I haven't seen you in two days. I aim to take my time with you."

The thought sent a hot little shiver rocketing down her spine. Cade, she'd discovered, preferred to make love at a turtle's pace. He also liked driving her crazy, making her writhe in sweet agony.

"No, I mean"—she caught his chin, turning his head until his gaze met hers—"*the couch*. That was always where…"

She blushed, unable to make herself finish the sentence. Maybe she shouldn't have told him that. It had to be pathetic to admit she usually masturbated on her living room couch. That she did wasn't sexy at all. It was needy and desperate.

Two lengthy strides past the couch, he came to a dead halt, staring at her for the span of a heartbeat, then jerked his head in the direction of the living room. "On the couch? Really?"

She had to be beet red by now, because her face was on fire. "I just always ended up there. I waited for you some nights."

His intense gaze seared into her, but she couldn't bring herself to look at him. She didn't want to know how pathetic he thought she was.

Cade's nose nudged her earlobe, his breath warm on her neck.

"Me too. I spend my days looking forward to coming home just so I can talk to you. Most of the time, I didn't even bother taking off my tie. If you weren't home, I waited." He turned and strode around the couch, then took a seat, depositing her in his lap. His soft lips skimmed the side of her neck, big hands sliding over her curves. His cock pushed into her ass, hard as granite in his pants. "I like the thought of you on this couch, fucking yourself with your fingers while thinking of me."

A hot shudder raked through her. A soft, serrated breath left her mouth. God, the man could talk her right out of her panties.

He scraped the skin where her neck met her shoulder. "Let's make new memories on this couch, baby."

She nodded, breathless, unable to deny she wanted, craved, and needed him to be inside of her. Now. God help her, but she needed the connection to him, to feel him with her, real and solid. It had been two days, but right then, it seemed a lifetime. She only had him for two weeks and she wanted as much of him as she could get before he went home and this ended.

They both moved at the same time, a desperate rush of activity as they attempted to shed enough clothing to come together. Cade pushed the front of his pants down enough to release his cock, then pulled a condom from the pocket of his pajamas. His gaze locked on her, eyes at half-mast and searing into her as he rolled the condom in place.

Hannah stood and shed her pajama bottoms, leaving them wadded on the floor at the base of the couch, then straddled his thighs. She locked her arms around his neck, buried her fingers in his thick hair, and sank onto him in one greedy stroke. Shivers raced across the surface of her sensitized skin.

His big warm hands closed around the globes of her bottom, his fingers digging into her skin, guiding their rhythm. Every sweet rocking of their hips rubbed her aching clit against his pelvis, and every thrust hurled her closer to the luscious abyss. She'd craved him all damn night. His thick cock buried inside of her, pumping hard into her. His big, soft hands sliding over her skin. Her body came alive beneath his touch, goose bumps popping up along her arms. So aroused, she already hung on the edge, already teetering.

His gaze never once left hers. The need and hunger in his eyes held her an all-too-willing captive. Something territorial flashed there, and something primal in her responded, her body rocking, thrusting harder against him even as his hands tightened on her ass, pulling her into him.

Her orgasm rushed up out of nowhere with a soundless *pop, pop, pop*. She gasped, bit her lower lip, and dropped her head back. A heady tidal wave washed over her, drowning her in bone-melting pleasure. She gasped and sighed in his lap. Beneath her, Cade's fingers bit into the flesh of her ass, his body shaking against her.

When the luscious quaking stopped, to be replaced by tiny aftershocks as her body came down from the rafters, she laid her forehead on his shoulder and tried to catch her breath. Cade wrapped his arms tight around her, and they sat for long moments holding each other in the aftermath.

When their breathing returned to normal, he turned his head and kissed the side of her neck, murmuring against her skin. "Hold on to me."

She did, tightening her arms around his shoulders, because

right then, she couldn't bring herself to let go. Hands on her bottom, he stood. His cock still buried inside of her, he carried her around the couch to the bedroom, slipping from her as he laid her on the bed.

In the darkness, with nothing but the streetlights beyond her window to light the room, he brushed a tender kiss across her mouth. "I'll be right back."

He disappeared into the attached bathroom, returning a few minutes later. He shed his shoes and his clothing, then climbed in beside her, rolled her on her side, and curled around her, his body warm against her back.

How long they lay in silence, she didn't know, but despite her orgasm, she still couldn't sleep. Cade's body had yet to relax behind her.

Finally, his lips brushed the back of her neck and his arm tightened around her waist, drawing her closer. "That secret I promised I'd share with you?"

She found his hand and curled her fingers over his. "Yeah?"

He hesitated a moment, his body tensing against her back, then drew a breath and released it in a rush. "I have a son."

His words were a bare murmur in the darkness. He'd told her the first day they met that he'd share when he was ready. Apparently, today was that day, and she took his confession for the gift it was. He spoke casually, as if he told her about his day, but the knowledge slid over her, an aching realization she could no longer deny. Over the last six months, they'd done this often, sharing triumphs, fears, disappointments. Things they might not have admitted to anyone else, but the space between them had always been sacred. It was easy talking to a faceless person, someone you knew you'd never meet. There was anonymity in it, a sense of safety.

She was awed that he'd share such an intimate detail with her, but her heart clenched all the same. The unbearable realization of exactly where she'd gotten herself settled over her. Oh for sure, he'd break her heart when he went home in a week and a half. After all, they were nothing more than temporary stops in each other's lives, a physical connection to make up for the lack they each felt in their lives. In the end, though, they'd still part ways. He'd go home, taking a piece of her with him, and she'd let him, because she needed the same from him in return.

The problem was, she had a feeling she'd miss him. Terribly. The thought filled her with questions she wasn't sure she wanted the answers to. Would their relationship change? Would they become distant and eventually drift apart? Or would it go back to the way it was? She didn't know. She didn't know what, exactly, she wanted, either. Only that as she lay in the shelter of his embrace, she felt close to him, and an emotion she didn't want to name or face twisted in her chest. Something that felt a lot like the first stirrings of love.

Neither could she ignore the pull of the intimacy his admission created between them.

She stroked her hand along his arm, his skin warm and the thick hairs soft beneath her fingers. "Tell me about him."

He took a breath, as if he'd been holding it, and the tension drained from his body. It occurred to her what his admission must have meant to him. Like her scar, it was something he'd held back, something close to his heart, and he feared her reaction, the same way she had.

She threaded her fingers with his, hoping to somehow show him what she didn't have the words to say. To show him she understood.

He pressed another soft kiss to the back of her neck before settling again. "When I was seventeen, I got a girl pregnant. She didn't want to keep the baby. She told me she wanted an abortion. Unplanned or not, that baby was half mine. Part of *me*. I managed to talk her into putting the baby up for adoption instead. In the end, the adoptive mother agreed to an open adoption, so long as I agreed not to interfere with his life. She sends me pictures, letters with updates on how he is. He's thirteen now."

Her heart twisted as her mind filled with what it must have cost him. A teenage pregnancy, then having to face giving up his child. Being forced to choose. It explained why he'd freaked the first time he'd forgotten to wear a condom, when they'd made love in the tub in his hotel room.

She squeezed his fingers in reassurance. "You miss him."

He grunted in agreement. "I was young and immature. My father insisted we give up the baby. I didn't know enough to argue. My father is domineering. I know he means well, but he makes decisions and he expects you to follow them without question. I always have. And the more I thought about it, the more I had to admit he was right. I could barely take care of myself let alone a baby, but he and my girlfriend forced me to choose, and I hated them for it. It's why I got the tat. My father hated it, but the ink is a part of me, the same way Ethan is.

"That's his name. Ethan Alexander. He's five-ten already. Strong and smart. He looks like me. In the end, I did what I thought was best for him at the time. I got to meet the birth parents, to help choose. That was part of my acceptance. I wanted a say in where he went. And I liked her. She has a good heart."

His choice of words didn't escape her notice. *At the time.*

"But now? If you could do it over, would you do it differently?"

He released a heavy breath, the air stirring the soft hairs on the back of her neck. "Honestly? I don't know. The adoptive mother is a wonderful woman. She tells me all the time how grateful she is I gave him to her. She can't have children. She and her husband tried for years, but they were never successful. He's the light of her life, and she's an excellent mother. I can't begrudge her that. She tells me that when Ethan's old enough, if he wants to know, she'll give him my contact information. For now, it's enough I get to watch him grow up."

She squeezed his arm in support. The pain and regret in his voice made her chest ache. "But you still miss him. I can hear it in your voice. You have regrets."

"Mmm. I can't help wondering if I did the right thing, if I should have fought harder to keep him." He was silent a moment; then his mouth nuzzled her neck, soft and distracted. His voice lowered to a vulnerable murmur against her skin. "I wanted him. Now I wonder if he'll hate me when he finds out, and I'm not sure I'd blame him if he did. Part of me is jealous. She gets things I'll never have. All those small, day-to-day things. Smiles. Hugs. He's *my* son. He wouldn't exist without me, but I'm a stranger to him. She gets to tuck him into bed at night and watch him sleep. Those are things I can't reconcile."

Her heart ached for him. "Did you ever get to hold him? Before they handed him over?"

"Once. Right after he was born. They offered the same to the mother, but she didn't want to see him. She didn't want him at all, but his adoptive mother let me hold him. He was so tiny, but so perfect. He had a full head of dark hair." Cade went silent for a moment, tension wafting off his body. After a moment, he released a heavy breath. "I think my heart claimed him, because letting him go was the hardest thing I've ever done. I almost took it back, changed my mind and my father be damned. But the look on the adoptive mother's face as she watched me. She had this anxiousness in her eyes, like maybe she knew what I was thinking. Or had the same fear. And I just knew he'd be okay."

This time, she couldn't resist the pull, the need to somehow take his pain or soothe the raw wound. Hannah rolled over to face him. The room lay in darkness but there was enough light to make out his features. He was a shadow within a shadow, his eyes dark hollows within his face, but his gaze seared into her. She didn't have to ask to know he waited for her reaction. He'd laid his heart out before her, and she couldn't begin to tell him what that meant to her.

So, she caressed his cheek. His stiff stubble prickled her skin, course yet soft. "Thank you. For sharing, I mean."

His hand slid over the curve of her hip to her bottom and he rolled onto his back, drawing her against his side. "I do a lot of things I probably shouldn't when I'm with you."

She settled her head into the crook of his shoulder and slid her hand over his stomach. "Such as?"

His hand squeezed her bottom playfully and his tone lightened.

"Such as coming over at midnight in my pajamas because I have to see you." He lifted his head, tucked his fingers beneath her chin and tipped her face to his, murmuring against her mouth as he sought hers in the darkness. He kissed her, the tender play of his lips over hers, then wrapped his arms tighter around her. "I'm addicted to you, Hannah Miller."

His voice came as a husky murmur in the darkness, and an answering shudder swept down her spine.

"Ditto." She kissed his chest then laid her head on the curve of his shoulder. His heartbeat had evened out, no longer erratic, nervous thumping, but a quiet, soothing pulse. The sound, along with the safety of his arms around her, lulled her, and in the comfortable silence, the old familiar memories rose. The dull, familiar ache throbbed in her chest and the need to share hit her hard. She shouldn't. What she ought to do was reinforce those boundaries, but neither could she stop the words from leaving her mouth. He'd shared with her, and she couldn't resist doing the same.

The way it always was with him when they talked. He lulled her into a sense of safety that scared the crap out of her. Because Cade had never felt like a stranger, but someone she'd known forever.

"After my parents died, I bounced around from foster home to foster home. Some were nice. Some weren't. When I was sixteen, they sent me to a group home. They had strict rules we had to follow. When meals were served, quiet time at night, curfew and bedtime. They even made sure we showered every day and took turns with the chores. Not everybody was nice. Some of the kids had been there nearly all their lives. Stuff got stolen. Fights happened. Bullies picked on the weaker, smaller kids. The usual kid stuff."

His hands swept over her in a lazy, mindless fashion, up and down her back, over the curve of her hip and up her side, fingertips occasionally following her spine. It told her in no uncertain terms he listened. She couldn't deny the gestures soothed her. Nor could she deny talking to him felt as right as rain. Over the six months since they met on that message board, Cade had become an intimate confidante. When she met him at the Space Needle, she hadn't been sure what to expect, but lying in the dark in the shelter of his embrace, sharing her world, however painful it might have been at times, was the most natural thing in the world.

So she gave in to the lure. In a week and a half, this would end and they'd go back to…something, but their relationship, this intimacy would end. Now, she couldn't resist. She needed this.

She slid a hand over his lean stomach, let her fingers wander through the dusting of dark hair there. "It's funny. Some parts of my life are a blur, a vague snapshot here and there. Like the accident. It's bits and pieces now. I'm not even sure I remember what my mother looks like anymore. The memories of her, of my parents, have faded. They're vague blips in my mind, a feeling more so than a specific memory. But I remember everything about the group home I lived in, the house. I remember every single face that came and went. The shenanigans we used to get into. The meals. Even the musty smell of the house."

"I don't think moments like those ever leave you."

His voice rumbled beneath her ear, his tone thoughtful but nonjudgmental. She nodded, her head rocking against his shoulder, grateful for his attentive ear, to know he not only listened, but also that he cared. "A couple of times you asked me to trust you, to learn to open up and talk to you. It makes you nervous that you think I don't."

"Sorry. It's a habit. One too many people have kept secrets from me. It's how I usually learned I was being used. People who are honest are open."

"And your ex wasn't."

His fingers trailed up her spine this time, leaving goose bumps in their wake. "Mmm."

"Truth is, I don't talk much about my life after my parents died because I learned not to over the years. The kids at school all talked about their parents, their siblings, complained about getting grounded. Normal stuff, you know? In the group home, nobody ever talked, at least not about anything except when they were getting out. I didn't want anybody to know I lived that way. What they don't tell you is that when you turn eighteen, you age out of the system and they let you go. Once you're an adult, you're on your own and you have to leave."

For a moment, only the sound of his quiet breathing echoing through his chest filled the aching silence rising over the room. Her chest tightened as she waited.

"So, you've been on your own since they died. What on earth did you do after you left the group home?"

She released her held breath, her body relaxing. She couldn't begin to tell him what it meant to know he listened and cared. Her chest swelled with the need to share her gratitude with him, but the words wouldn't come. They were stuck in the rising lump forming in her throat.

Instead, she snuggled closer and simply answered his question. "My parents left me a trust. They gave it to me when I turned eighteen. I lived off of it. Got a job and an apartment. Went to school."

"That's pretty admirable, putting yourself through school."

She shrugged. "I only knew I didn't want to end up back where I'd been. I lived on the streets for a couple of weeks after they let me go, and I knew I wanted more than that. One of the memories I have is my mother telling me, 'Don't ever let anybody tell you that you can't do or be something. You can be whatever you set your mind to.'"

Her mother's words had stuck, had been the driving force in her life. Her parents had given their lives, and she'd ended up in a sometimes dysfunctional place, but those words had gotten her through.

"When did you open the bookstore?"

"About three years ago. I met Maddie at a midsized publishing house I worked at for a couple of years. I worked as an editorial assistant. She worked in marketing. It's what she does at the shop. She's good at it. One day, she suggested we open a bookstore together. I've always loved books. They're what got me through. As a girl, I always had my nose in a book."

He growled, a sexy little rumble in the back of his throat. His warm palm slid over her bare backside. "Reading is sexy."

Recognizing her own sentiment, she let out a quiet laugh and echoed his earlier response.

"I'm glad you think so. My mother worked as a librarian, and reading always made me feel closer to her. I've always collected old books, the ones I treasured the most. Maddie and I got to looking through my collection one day, and she offhandedly suggested I open a shop." She let out a quiet laugh. "I have an English degree I don't use."

"I think you just described half the people who graduate college. I know a few who ended up in professions they didn't go to school for." His arms tightened around her. "Tell me about your parents."

Hannah relaxed into his side, listening to the soothing *thumb-bump* of his heartbeat, and surrendered to the lull between them. They spent the next several hours talking. She told him things she'd sworn once she wouldn't ever tell anyone. The things she remembered about her parents. The first few years after she opened the shop, when she feared the business would fail. Even some of the painful secrets of living in foster care. In return, he shared bits and pieces of himself. His son. His twin sister, Christina. His mother, who forever tried to fix him up with the single women who ran in their circles.

On a return trip from the bathroom, the time on the clock caught her. Seated on the edge of the bed, she stared at the red numbers: 3:04 a.m. She shouldn't allow him to stay. She'd made that particular rule. The need to kick him out wouldn't surface, though, no matter how much she told herself she needed to stick to the script. She had to admit, she enjoyed lying there with him. Something as simple as lying in the dark sharing her life with him gave her more than the great sex. She'd give up the entire two weeks for another night like this, to lie in his arms and talk, luxuriate in the intimacy and closeness.

"I know I'm the one who made the rule, but…" She swallowed, her voice lowering with the vulnerability sliding over her. "You don't have to leave."

He let out a quiet chuckle behind her. "Good. I hadn't planned on it."

She turned her head to look at him. The light from outside provided enough illumination to make out the dark shape of his face. She couldn't be positive, but she swore he grinned at her.

Her own mouth lifted in response. "A bit sure of yourself, there, GQ."

"Nope. Just hopeful. Come back to bed." His hand found hers in the darkness, and he tugged her to him. When she lay down beside him again, he lifted his head, his mouth finding hers. His lips moved with a lazy languidness, plying and tugging, as if he had all the time in the world.

She melted into the warm, moist slide of his mouth and shifted to lie along his length. A contented sigh left her and warning bells blared a red alert in her head. She was in trouble. She was in a damn lot of it. Four days in, and she'd already broken her own rule. Like the wondrous pull of a good book, Cade McKenzie had hooked her. God help her, but she couldn't put him down.

Chapter Seven

As the sunrise chased the shadows from the room the next morning, Cade lay on his side, one arm tucked beneath his pillow. He'd been awake for twenty minutes now. Beside him, Hannah still slept. She hadn't moved much during the night. She had to be the only woman he'd ever been with who didn't take over the entire bed, covers and all. She'd rolled over, but otherwise, she kept to her position, lying on her side, breathing softly.

She looked the way she had when she'd gone to sleep. No wild, tangled mane of bed head. No morning raccoon eyes. She'd taken her makeup off sometime last night while he slept. He had the first glimpse of her *au naturel*. Her beauty took his breath away. She had almond-shaped eyes, flawless skin, and full, rosy lips he had the desire to lean over and taste.

This two-week affair had been his idea, the rules half his, but lying there, watching her sleep, he couldn't deny the emotion throbbing in his chest anymore. The thought of going back to his condo in San Diego and never seeing her like this again tied his heart in knots.

Hannah scared the hell out of him. He'd tried so hard the last two days to redraw his boundaries, to put her back in the proper box, but his time with her dwindled day by day. He had a week and a half left. Ten days to enjoy her. Then what? He'd go back to sleeping alone? To days, weeks, months spent burying himself up to his eyeballs in work so he wouldn't have to feel the loneliness pulsing inside of him?

It was what he wanted once. The old man had high expectations and something in Cade responded, wanted to meet them. He enjoyed the challenge, yet yearned to prove to his father he'd grown up, that he wasn't that seventeen-year-old kid who'd carelessly gotten a girl pregnant.

He'd convinced himself work provided everything he needed, but time with Hannah had made him realize how empty his life had become and how much he wanted more. Amelia had been another expectation met. He'd convinced himself he'd fallen in love with her, but now, lying there, watching Hannah sleep, the truth stared him in the face. Amelia hadn't made him feel even half the way Hannah did. Hannah set him free. She accepted him at face value and he could be himself. No name, no obligations, no expectations.

That's where he'd gotten stuck. He didn't know what happened now. He'd spent his life building what he had, and so had she. Never mind they'd agreed their relationship was a fling—short-lived and destined to end. They couldn't be any farther apart from each other.

She stirred beside him, her eyelids fluttering open, and rolled onto her back, stretching her hands over her head and yawning. When her gaze landed on him, she dropped her arms and smiled, surprise lighting her eyes. "You're still here."

"That particular rule was yours, not mine." He winked, then rolled over on top of her, holding himself on his elbows as he settled between her thighs. God, how he loved the way she fit against him. He brushed a kiss across her alluring mouth. "Sleep well?"

One thing he *did* know. All she had to do was smile at him, and he wanted her. His cock throbbed to life, settling against the hot folds of her body. He wanted to make love to her one last time before he had to leave her for the day. He wanted a piece of her to take with him.

"Like a baby." She purred low in her throat and bent her knees, cradling his hips with her thighs. Her hands slid up his back, and she arched against him. The head of his cock slid inside her.

Cade let out a low, agonized groan. He wanted more than anything to follow her lead, to push into her to the hilt and make love to her until she screamed his name. The way her body responded to his blew his damn mind. He couldn't get enough of her.

He nipped at her bottom lip. "Hold that thought, baby."

He moved off her long enough to pull the last condom from the pocket of his pajama bottoms—because he didn't go anywhere without being prepared—then rejoined her. She slid her hands up his back, gathering him close, her ankles locking around his hips as he slid into her. He rested there a moment, enjoying the luscious pull of her body around him, gripping him like a warm, wet glove.

"Christ, you feel good. So hot and wet." He pressed a kiss to her lips and slid all the way out, inch by aching inch, then pushed all the way back in the same way. He wanted to prolong their time together. He'd have to go soon and he wanted as much of her as he could get before obligation made him leave her.

"I dreamt about you." Hannah gasped. Her nails scraped the backs of his shoulders. Her hips arched, rising to meet his slow thrust.

Cade took his time. He allowed himself to enjoy the moment and watching the lazy bliss travel across her features. She clutched his back and wrapped her body around his, her hips rocking in time with his. His every cell focused on her. Her quiet moans. Her harsh, erratic breathing, and the little purrs emanating from the back of her throat.

He slid a hand beneath her ass, changed the angle, and Hannah erupted beneath him. She gasped, her thighs clamped around his hips, her body convulsing beneath him and around him, pulling a lazy, exquisite orgasm from him. He followed on her heels, hips jerking as he came.

He dropped his head into the crook of her shoulder, drowning himself in her scent. Hannah didn't release her hold on him, either, but rather tightened her grip. He rolled onto his side and wrapped his arms around her in return. She rested her head on his chest and they lay together for long minutes in silence, holding each other, both of them continuing to shake.

When his breathing returned to normal, he lifted his head, meeting her gaze. He tucked her hair behind her ear with the tip of his index finger. Why was leaving her so damn difficult? This was only supposed to be a fling, but something about her spoke to something in him. He wanted to stay, to spend the day wrapped around her, doing things like eating finger foods in bed. He wanted to make her laugh, to watch her smile light up her eyes.

Which was why he needed to leave. "I have to go."

She nodded, but didn't otherwise say anything. Unable to resist, he brushed his mouth over hers, one last taste to take with him during the day. Her lips opened beneath his, their breath mingling. Her body reached for him in turn, surging to meet him.

Yeah. They'd reached *that* point. They were comfortable touching, but not yet comfortable with the kind of needing that had nothing to do with the physical body. No, this had everything to do with something they'd agreed had no place in their exchanges—emotion. It was there nonetheless. They'd reached the point where emotion began to trickle in and reason began to trickle out. He'd been here before, when he thought he'd fallen in love with Amelia.

He forced himself to pull back, to shift off her and get out of bed. He went into the attached bathroom to get rid of the condom, then found his clothing on the floor and pulled it on. He could only shake his head at himself as he did. Pajamas. He'd come over in pajamas. That was a first. He'd never needed someone so much he let all decorum slide.

Hannah didn't follow suit. Instead, she rolled onto her side and propped herself on an elbow, watching him with eyes hooded by an emotion he didn't want to look too closely at. After he dressed, he went back to the bed, braced his hands on either side of her, and pressed a goodbye kiss to her lips. The pull of her mouth once again sucked all reason from his mind. She melted beneath him, and he leaned into her, taking more than the simple peck he'd intended.

Breathing hard now, he pulled back, closed his eyes, and surrendered, resting his forehead against hers. "God, you drive me crazy. I don't want to leave."

"I don't want you to leave either."

The quiet vulnerability in her voice made him open his eyes. Her gaze darted over his face. The anxiousness there matched the knots in his stomach. They'd gotten caught in something that terrified him, because he wanted it. He wanted everything her gorgeous eyes promised him. The intimacy, the sweet connection. He knew without a doubt she could fill all those empty spaces.

He pressed another kiss to her lips, then forced himself to straighten. "I'm in meetings all day, but I should be done by six. Meet me at the hotel?"

She nodded, and he winked at her, then turned and left the room, every bit as conflicted as when he'd shown up on her doorstep last night. He had a decision to make. He could either take a step forward, toward her, or put more effort into redrawing his boundaries. The question was, what did he want? Was he ready to set his heart on the line?

* * *

By the time his day ended and six o'clock rolled around, he wasn't one step closer to making his decision. It had been a long day of contract negotiations. This merger should have been easy, but the two companies were still arguing, and his head throbbed.

He looked forward to Hannah, more than he should. His heart had a definite mind of its own and it wanted her. He had a sinking feeling he was already halfway to falling in love with her.

A knock sounded on the hotel room door and his heart skipped a beat like he was seventeen all over again. Which then made his gut knot. It couldn't be good when he anticipated and feared seeing Hannah with equal measure. He'd open the door, take one look at her, and be inside her five minutes later for all the self-control he possessed with her. He craved her like he craved coffee in the morning, and there wasn't anything he didn't like about her. She was real and breathtakingly honest.

His heart still skipped a beat, though, desire already coursing through him as he strode to the door. His smile plastered itself across his face as he undid the locks and pulled the door open. "Hey, gorgeous."

Cade froze. The woman on the other side of the threshold wasn't Hannah. Rather, his sister, Christina, stood in the quiet hallway, hands folded in front of her, little blue purse tucked beneath her left arm. Her long dark hair hung loose down her back, and she wore a simple black pencil skirt and a white blouse. Neat and perfect as always. At the sight of him, she smiled. Green eyes so much like his glittered with amusement.

"Hey, yourself." She didn't wait for an invitation, as usual, but pushed past him into the suite. "You haven't called me, Caden. Mom sent me to make sure you were still alive."

His hope sank as he turned, watching her stride into the suite's living room. He poked his head out the door, but the hallway stood empty and quiet. No Hannah. Disappointment surged through him, and with a resigned sigh, he closed the door and followed his sister.

Standing beside the coffee table, Chris arched an elegantly curved brow. "Expecting someone?"

He didn't miss the amusement in her gaze. An M.I.T. graduate, his sister had an eye for detail. She didn't miss much. So he smiled. He hadn't seen her in a while. He and Chris didn't keep secrets. They told each other everything and always had. He always knew she'd be on his side, no matter what. Despite that, Hannah ought to be here any minute, and he had no desire to explain their relationship to Chris. He didn't think he had the words.

"Nobody. Only a dinner companion." He moved to her side and wrapped her in a hug. He had to admit he *was* glad to see her. She was the only other woman alive who didn't expect anything from him.

She pulled back, her eyes filling with mischief. The look meant one thing—she was about to go on a fishing expedition.

She patted his chest. "You haven't had a date since you broke it off with Amelia. Spill it."

"I love you, Chris, but you're not getting details." He kissed her forehead, then released her. "What brings you by?"

She stared at him for a moment, then moved to the couch and took a seat, crossing one long leg over the other. "You haven't called me. We were supposed to have lunch when you got into town. Or did you forget?"

Recalling the exact conversation two weeks ago, guilt slid through him. Cade stuffed his hands in his pockets and nodded absently. "Mmm. I'm sorry. I've been a bit distracted this week."

Her eyes lit up like the sun. She giggled with glee, not unlike a child presented with a room full of new toys, and sat forward on the couch. "At least tell me her name."

This time he couldn't help but laugh. She was nosy, but she always did it with so much joy he could never hold it against her. His sister was among the few women who didn't have ulterior motives. With her, what you saw was you got. She was honest and kindhearted, and she worried about him.

He shook his head. "You're not getting details. Who I date is nobody's business but mine."

Chris's face fell, hurt rising in her eyes. "Even me?"

Cade heaved a breath and took a seat beside her, wrapping an arm around her. She laid her head on his shoulder. "I love you to the moon and back. You're a part of me. But this stuff? Mom gets wind of this, and I'll never hear the end of it. I want something just for me, and she's it."

She tipped her head back in order to meet his gaze. "I'm glad you're seeing someone, though. You need it. You can't stop living."

Feeling trapped by this particular conversation, Cade pushed off the couch and moved to the windows. He watched a couple of boats whir through the water below. "Don't start. It's only been seven months. It's not like I've become a hermit."

"But it's not like you, Caden. You've had a girl on your arm for as long as I can remember."

She had a point. He sighed. "Because Mom expected it of me. She introduces me to half the damn universe. She thinks it's time I settled down and started producing heirs and Dad agrees with her."

"That's just her way of saying she wants grandbabies. She tells me the same thing."

He shook off the gloom looming over him and looked back at her. "Don't you ever get tired of it? Having to pretend all the time? Never knowing who you can trust and who you can't?"

Chris let out a heavy sigh.

"Yes. I am. I got a kick out of it in college. It was a little harmless fun to play with the ones who thought I had no clue. Now I'm thirty-one, and it's a lonely place to be." She pushed off the couch, coming to stand beside him, and leaned her head against his shoulder. "Tell me one thing. This girl you won't tell me about, is she one of them?"

Cade shook his head. "Not even close. Mom would never approve of her. She doesn't have any money or family. She's down to earth and simple. It's what I like so much about her. She doesn't expect anything from me. She takes me as I am."

"I'm glad. You deserve to be happy, little brother."

Cade resisted the urge to roll his eyes. Little brother. Chris had been lording that over him for most of their lives, that she was the older twin.

Letting the nickname slide, he turned his head, peering at her. "So do you."

Chris flashed a gentle smile. "And I will be. *I* haven't given up. At least not completely. Have you heard anything regarding the lawsuit with Amelia?"

He made a noncommittal sound and turned back to watching the water. Whenever he came to the city, he preferred to stay here. He loved the view. Something about the water and all the trees in the distance filled him with a sense of peace he always wished he could take home with him. Now Hannah gave him that feeling. Too bad he couldn't take *her* home with him.

"No. She still hasn't complied. We're filing a motion to have her held in contempt of court." He glanced down at his sister and arched a brow. "Is that all you came over for? To berate me for not dating?"

Chris let out a quiet laugh and pushed off his shoulder. "No. I had a reason, though I'm not sure you'll like it now."

A miserable groan escaped him. Chris had taken up their mother's pastime. She seemed to have inherited the matchmaking gene. "What did you do?"

Chris flashed a sheepish grin. "The breast cancer charity auction is in a few days."

Cade narrowed his gaze on her. "Uh-huh. And?"

"It's another bachelor auction this year. Last year's was such a success we decided to do it again, but we're short two bachelors. Two guys backed out at the last minute. Trevor Von Bosch had a family emergency, and Edward Lyle got engaged, of all things. I volunteered you and Baz."

Baz being his best friend, Sebastian Blake. They'd gone to school together. Christina was the only one who still called him by his childhood nickname.

Chris didn't have to say it. He knew what was coming and the repercussions filled his mind. His sister headed the local charity for breast cancer research. It was a charity their family believed in and donated generously to every year. Chris had cornered him last year as well, talking him into allowing her to put him on the auction block. The prize was, of course, a date with each bachelor.

Cade closed his eyes, exhausted and overwhelmed by the

prospect before him. "Oh, tell me you didn't. Tell me Mom didn't send you."

"No, this was mine. I thought it would do you some good." She laid her hand on his shoulder, her fingers soft and warm. "You spend too much time alone. You and Baz still aren't speaking, so you haven't been spending time with him. You don't have a girl."

He couldn't argue with her there. He couldn't even be angry with her for not asking him first, either. Unlike their mother, Chris's concern had less to do with marrying him off than filling a need she somehow saw lacking within him. Fraternal or not, he'd shared a womb with her, and she knew him better than almost anyone.

He sighed and opened his eyes. She stared at him, a worried frown creasing her brow. "I know you mean well, but you have to trust me to find my own way. I was an awkward kid, but never helpless. You have to stop fixing."

Another knock sounded on the suite door. His gaze shot to the door, his heart sinking into his toes. He released a heavy breath. The news he had to share with Hannah weighed on him.

Chris touched his arm. "Tell me."

"I made her a promise I'm going to have to break." He'd have to look Hannah in the face and tell her he had to break a rule. Any other time, obligation would make this decision easy. After all, he and Chris had gone to these fund-raisers every year since they were kids, and every year their father made a large donation. That this year's was another bachelor auction provided a complication. Given everything he and Hannah had talked about, however, he had a sneaking suspicion this particular rule meant the most to her. "I don't look forward to telling her I'm going to have to date someone else."

Chris studied him for a moment, searching something in his face, then hiked her chin and straightened her shoulders. She strode past him with a decisive nod. "Then I'll do it. I made this mess. I'll clean it up."

* * *

Hannah's stomach did a flip. The silence of the hallway around her did nothing for the frazzled state of her nerves. Insane. She had to be insane for doing this.

She glanced down, recinched the tie of her overcoat for the thousandth time, then looked back at the door and drew a deep breath. Of all the things she'd ever done, this had to be the boldest. The idea and execution had been Maddie's. Hell, even the tan overcoat belonged to her braver-than-her redheaded best friend.

They'd spent the afternoon in a lingerie store Hannah would never have gone into alone. The kind with the naughty stuff sitting beside the vibrators and dildos. Shoot, if it weren't for Maddie's pep talk, she never would have left her apartment this way. She bought her vibrators online. Anonymously. Never in her life had she walked the streets of downtown Seattle in a garter belt, stockings, and fuck-me-red stilettos.

And little else.

When she'd left her apartment, she'd floated on top of the world. She had to hand it to Maddie. She *felt* sexy as hell, something that didn't happen often, and the thought of Cade's reaction had her simmering on a low boil.

Standing here, staring at his hotel room door, however, the luscious warmth that had settled low in her belly when she left her apartment had faded to a cold chill. What if he hated it?

Memories filled her thoughts. A young man's cruel laughter rang in her head. *"Attracted to you? Oh, that's rich."*

Maddie's words to her a half hour ago followed on the heels of the old, painful memory. *"Would you stop worrying? You look phenomenal. No man in his right mind would turn you down, and you know damn well he thinks you're sexy. Walk tall, girlfriend, because you are smokin."*

Hannah drew a deep breath for courage, drew her shoulders back, and knocked on the door again.

"I'll get it. I created this mess. I'll clean it up."

The soft, feminine voice coming from within the room drew Hannah up short.

"Uh-uh. You open that door, and she's going to flip."

She recognized Cade's voice. The feminine voice, however, caught her in the chest. Hannah froze. Panic clawed its way through her, setting her heart pounding in immediate denial of the thoughts flying through her mind. Namely, who on earth was the woman in Cade's room?

No. Cade wouldn't do that to her. Surely he had a logical explanation.

Or so she told herself. One too many excuses from Dane echoed through her mind. So, too, did his speech the last time she saw him, when he confessed he'd been seeing someone else for more than a few months. Her mind filled with every excuse every guy looking to back out of a date had ever fed her. All her fears collapsed on top of her. How much did she know about

Cade, really? She'd taken him at face value, assuming he told her the truth. What if he hadn't? Okay, so they'd agreed it would be just sex, but she hadn't agreed to be another someone's joke…

The door finally opened to reveal a stunning brunette. She stood several inches over Hannah's meager five foot three, with long dark hair falling in lush waves past her shoulders. She also had a perfect figure, no doubt a puny size six. Her slender legs went clear up to her ears, and her breasts were well more than a handful. Hannah wanted to shrink back. Whatever her relationship to Cade, this woman was everything Hannah yearned to be.

Cade moved up the hallway behind the woman, his strides long and determined, panic in his eyes.

Fear clogged her throat. Denial rang in her mind. Hannah looked between the two of them, waiting for someone to let her off the hook, for Cade to tell her she had it wrong, that it wasn't what it looked like. She took a step back, confusion waging war with the past, but Cade's hand shot out, catching her wrist and stopping her retreat. His eyes pleaded with her.

"No, no, no. Don't you dare think it. I would never do that to you." He turned his head, brow furrowed, and nudged the woman beside him with an elbow. "Go ahead, Miss 'I'll clean up this mess.' Introduce yourself. You're getting me in serious hot water. You need to learn to call first and stop barging in."

The woman turned her head, glaring back at him. "How was I supposed to know you'd have a girl in your room?"

Cade rolled his eyes. "Will you introduce yourself already?"

The woman turned back to Hannah and smiled again, this one friendly and apologetic.

"I'm so sorry to intrude on your date. If my brother here"—the woman shot an irritated glance in Cade's direction—"had told me he had a girlfriend, I might have known to call before coming over. Caden tends to isolate, and I thought…"

The woman continued to chatter, but Hannah's mind stopped listening. Two words lodged themselves in her brain and stuck there: *girlfriend* and *brother*. Understanding began to dawn as Hannah took a moment to look over the woman across from her. She and Cade had the same black hair, the same mossy-green eyes set deep in the face, even the same wide mouth. The woman stood several inches shorter than him, of course, tall and slender to his broad and brawny, and her jaw had a more feminine curve to it, but the resemblance was there.

Hannah blew out her held breath, her shoulders slumping. "Oh my God. You're his sister."

Cade released her wrist. The tension radiating off him drained. "Hannah, this is Christina. Chris, Hannah Miller."

Christina extended a perfectly manicured hand, done in a neat French manicure. "Pleased to meet you."

Hannah forced a polite smile, praying it didn't look as uncomfortable as she felt, and took the woman's hand. "You as well."

As they shook, Christina's shrewd gaze took her in from head to toe; then she turned to Cade, braced a hand against his chest, and pushed him inside the room.

"We girls need a minute." Despite his surprised expression, she closed the door, leaving it unlatched enough to get back inside. Alone in the hallway, Christina's eyes lit up. She covered her mouth with her hands for a moment, taking Hannah in from head to toe again. Then Christina caught her in a hug so tight she almost couldn't breathe.

Christina's voice came as a whisper between them. "I'm sorry. I have to ask. Are you naked under there?"

Hannah's face heated a thousand degrees. Of all times for her to meet his family, it had to be now? She sighed. "Nearly. It was supposed to be a surprise. I'm so mortified. I'm sorry we had to meet this way."

"My fault. Caden's correct. I should have called. But I have to admit I'm so glad I didn't. It's wonderful to meet you. You're exactly what he needs. Since the fiasco that was his fiancée, he's been isolating himself. Mom and I have been worried. As for your surprise…" Christina pulled back, holding Hannah by the upper arms, and looked her over once and winked. "Caden won't know what hit him."

Hannah couldn't help herself. She bit her lower lip and looked down at herself. "I sure hope so. It was very nerve-wracking walking through downtown this way."

Christina covered her mouth and giggled behind her hand. "I did something similar once, except I was actually naked. I got caught on the way and had to sit through a meeting I'd forgotten about. I was beside myself. Never date someone you work with. Come on. Let's go let Caden off the hook. No doubt he's fuming on the other side of the door, ready to strangle me."

Christina took her hand and pushed the door open. Cade had been pacing a line between the living room and the end of the small foyer hallway. He halted halfway between and pivoted toward them, eyes shifty and anxious.

He arched a dark brow. "Everything okay?"

"Everything's great. I'm so glad I stopped by. It was nice meeting you, Hannah." Christina hugged her like they were old friends, then straightened and winked before pivoting toward her brother. She closed the distance between them, hugged his left shoulder, and lifted on her tiptoes to kiss his cheek.

"Lunch, Caden. You owe me lunch before you go home. I miss you. You're too much like Dad, always at work." She pulled back, one hand on his shoulder, head tipped back as she peered at him. "You sure you don't want me to tell her? It might sound better coming from me. After all, I made this mess. I'm so sorry, little brother. I was worried. I wanted something to pull you out of your funk, and it's always a fun night."

"You and Mom need to stop meddling. Mom wants *heirs*. Dad says I need a good wife, to put out a good image for the firm." Cade blew out a breath, and whatever irritation had crossed his features drained from him. "She's the first thing I've done for me in a long time. And, no, but thank you. I'd rather handle this one myself."

Christina patted his chest.

"Mom won't hear this from me, I promise." She kissed his cheek again, then turned and strode for the door. Once there, she pulled the door open, then paused and turned. Her bright expression fell, somberness filling her eyes. Eyes way too much like her brother's and every bit as expressive. "In case you didn't hear, Baz is back from Paris. You need to forgive him. Amelia used the both of you, pitted you against each other, for her own selfish gain. In the end, she lost. That's all that matters."

Once again Cade rolled his eyes like a petulant child. "Says the woman who won't admit she's in love with my best friend."

Christina rolled her eyes right back, but pink seeped into her cheeks, betraying her. "I'm not in love with Sebastian. The man is insufferable. I don't know what you two have in common, because you couldn't be more different. There isn't a shred of humility in him. He thinks way too highly of himself."

Laughter rumbled out of Cade. "You do realize he's that way because he knows it drives you crazy, right?"

"The point being"—Christina narrowed her eyes in warning—"she used him the same way she used you. The two of you are miserable without each other."

Cade folded his arms and arched a brow, amusement glittering in his eyes. "What's this about not being in love with him?"

She turned to Hannah and rolled her eyes.

"Sebastian and Caden have been joined at the hip since elementary school. They don't fight often, but when they do…stubborn as mules, the both of them. Neither one is ever willing to admit being at fault. They've always been that way, too. Whenever they fought, our nanny, MaryAnn, would force them to sit beside each other until they apologized. The fools would sit there for hours in stubborn refusal. Too much macho bravado that they're willing to let a woman get in the way of a lifelong friendship. A woman who didn't deserve either of them." She turned to Cade and pointed a stern finger. "Fix it, Caden, or you'll regret it. Hannah, I'm so sorry I intruded, but I'm glad we got to meet."

The door closed behind her with a soft click, leaving her and Cade alone.

Chapter Eight

Hannah remained frozen halfway up the hallway. Cade stood at the edge of the living room, hands tucked in his pockets. Several long moments passed in silence after his sister left, neither one moving. She didn't know what to say to him. Whatever bravado she'd sashayed over there with deserted her somewhere out in the hallway.

Cade stood stiff, his jaw set a little too tight. Hannah feared if she moved, something would break between them. Awkward tension and something she couldn't put her finger on, something in the stiff set of his shoulders, became a wall between them. Something clearly weighed on his mind. She wished he'd get it over with and tell her, because the tension was killing her.

Meeting his sister and getting a glimpse of his life had knocked her for a loop. Watching the two of them, she'd been an intruder on an intimate moment, but she had to admit their interaction had mesmerized her. She and Cade had shared a lot in their online chats, but his sister's appearance was the first glimpse at the intimate side of his life. His family. She had to admit, she liked seeing this side of him. Watching him with his twin sister had lodged something inside of her she feared naming, let alone acknowledging, a part of her she'd carried since her parents' death all those years ago. She envied him his relationship with Christina, and she wanted, more than she should, to see him in his world, to see the man in his element.

Cade had a soft side, a sister who cared about him. Hannah knew nothing about his world. She played little to no part in it. While the sex blew her mind, she longed to be a part of his world in a way she could no longer deny but that had terror settling cold and hard in her belly. Merely being his physical release at the end of the day seemed shallow now.

She longed for more. She longed for the family she hadn't had growing up. Oh, she had Maddie, and she would be forever grateful for that, but Maddie was *all* she had. She made sure of it. If she didn't let people in, they couldn't leave her. She'd learned that the hard way over the years. Never get attached, because they always left.

For the second time in her life, Cade had her pondering what she wanted from her life, deep down where it counted.

Cade broke the tense moment first. His gait relaxed, and he closed the distance between them, coming to a stop in front of her. "Hi."

His sexy, familiar scent swirled around her like a lure. His broad form made her shiver with heat and awareness of the man. He became a wall of muscle in front of her, all she could see and all she wanted to see. Her knees turned to gelatin, and in that small space, need flared between them. Only this morning, she'd woken in his arms, had looked forward all day to this moment right here, when she'd have him all to herself again. After everything that had gone on in the last half hour, the power of her need for him hit like a freight train.

She sagged back against the wall behind her. The man made her dizzy, drunk on the pull he had over her. "Hi, yourself."

He leaned into her and her troubled thoughts evaporated. His hands settled on her waist, and Hannah sighed in bliss.

"I'm sorry about that. I hadn't anticipated her coming over." One corner of his mouth lifted. "Chris has always taken on the role of the big sister, even when we were kids, though technically, she's only thirteen minutes older than I am. I honestly think it's a role she was born for, but she can be pushy sometimes."

The pink staining his cheeks had her smiling in spite of herself. He *was* nervous.

Unable to resist, she slid her hands up his chest, delighting in the muscle beneath her palms and the addicting heat of his body. "It's okay. I like her. She's nice."

He made a sound low in his throat and shook his head.

"Mmm. I love my sister, but she wasn't who I wanted to see right then." His gaze dropped. The tip of his index finger traced the lapels of her coat, following the seam between her breasts. "What do you have on under here?"

She drew a deep breath and released it. Drawing up her inner vixen, she fingered the lapels of the overcoat. "It's a present. For you. Unwrap me."

"It's not even my birthday." Amusement and heat warred in his gaze. He took a step back and untied the sash around her waist, then undid the buttons and pulled the sides of the coat open.

The bra she'd chosen had low-cut cups that didn't cover her nipples, but thrust her too-small breasts front and center. The cool air rushing over her skin made her nipples tighten and ache, but the bra did its job, for hunger flared in his eyes as his gaze raked over her.

He fingered the edge of the bra, the tip of his index finger brushing a hardened nipple. "Did you walk over here like this?"

She nodded, unable to help the shiver that coursed through her. "It was rather freeing. At least, until I got here."

Walking downtown, knowing she wore nothing more than a revealing bra, see-through panties, and fuck-me heels had filled her with a sexiness she didn't think she could ever match. At least until this moment. His eyes ate up every inch of her, and a flick of her gaze downward revealed a growing tent in his tailored slacks. For the first time in a long time, she *felt* sexy.

She arched a teasing brow. "You like?"

He made a quiet, contented *hmm*, and his large, warm hands slid over the curve of her hips to close over her ass. He lifted her off her feet like she weighed nothing and pressed her back against the wall. The length of his erection settled against her, hard as granite behind his zipper. His face a bare inch from hers, his eyes glittered with challenge and triumph and a scorching heat. "That about answer your question?"

She gasped, her hips pushing into the sweet pulse of him. The ridge of his erection rubbed the exact right spot, and Hannah shivered. "God, I was so nervous coming over here. I wasn't sure what you'd think. I've never worn lingerie like this for a man, the naughty stuff. When your sister opened the door, I thought I was going to die, but the look on your face made the effort worth it."

Cade went still as a statue. His countenance changed. The teasing, playful light gave way to something softer, more tender. His eyes searched hers for a moment before he bent his head, his hot mouth trailing a lazy path over the curve of her jaw, down her neck, and across her shoulder.

"You have no idea what you do to me, do you? I crave you like a junkie. You're all I think about. I need you. I've needed you since I left you this morning. Like I need to draw my next breath." He nipped the curve of her shoulder, then pressed his cheek hard against hers. His voice lowered to a vulnerable murmur against her ear. "You scare the hell out of me, Hannah."

His words echoed the feeling she'd had standing out in the hallway. Red alert blared in her head. She needed to end this here and now, leave while her heart remained intact. She'd broken a rule she spent her life upholding until Dane. Her ex only proved she should have upheld her promise to herself—never get attached. Cade's words confirmed what she already knew: they'd become caught in something not part of the deal.

Instead, her arms and legs tightened around him, drawing him closer. She couldn't stop trembling. Cade McKenzie overwhelmed her senses. She needed him the same way he needed her. Something she couldn't explain if she tried but couldn't deny either.

God help her heart when these two weeks ended.

Cade crushed her to him. He buried his face in her throat, his breathing harsh and ragged against her skin. How long they remained that way, clinging to each other, she didn't know, but it hadn't escaped her notice she wasn't the only one shaking.

With a deep breath, he pulled back. His expression took her

by surprise. She wasn't sure what she'd expected, tenderness maybe. Instead, his eyes searched her face anxiously.

"I'm afraid I have news, and I'd rather tell you now before we get too deep into this. As much as I hate to waste your surprise, I need to tell you something." He set her to her feet, stepped back, and held out a hand. "Take a bath with me?"

The worry staring back at her from his gaze caught her in the chest. Something weighed on him and the acknowledgment of it knotted her stomach.

She nodded, slipping her hand into his. "Is everything okay?"

He shook his head, his fingers closing almost painfully around hers.

"I don't know. That depends on you. Chris came over to drop a bomb on me." He drew a deep breath and released it before continuing. "I'm going to have to break a rule."

The anxiety written in his searching eyes had the same emotion swelling like a tide within her. Something deep inside tightened to painful proportions. Why did she get the feeling she was about to lose him?

Cade tied her heart in knots. She couldn't deny it anymore. She was falling in love with him.

"Bath." Hannah tightened her grip on his hand and stepped around him, pulling him behind her as she made her way toward the bathroom. "And wine. I want you naked before I hear this."

Outside the bathroom, Cade came to a dead halt, forcing her to stop along with him. "Baby, I think you should hear me out first."

His words and the regret in his tone made her insides shake.

He obviously worried she'd hate his news, and his worry had a lump forming in her throat.

She swallowed hard and turned to face him. She needed to be honest with him. "The expression on your face scares me. You're worried about something and it's never good when the man you're seeing says 'we need to talk.' I get this feeling something is about to interrupt our time together, and I don't mean just tonight. Am I right?"

His thumb swept along her wrist. "That depends on you."

She rolled her eyes, irritated with yet another elusive non-answer. "Will you stop saying that?"

He shook his head. "I'm sorry, but it's true. A familial obligation has crept up, one I hadn't anticipated, because my darling sister volunteered me without asking first. Carrying it out breaks a rule, one we both agreed was important."

She stared at him, blinked, processed. She didn't have to ask. Her sinking stomach told her which rule he meant: the one where they'd agreed not to see other people.

She sighed and released his hand. The weight of a thousand elephants sat upon her, pressing her down. Her shoulders rounded. Her outfit didn't feel sexy anymore, but more like a clown suit. "Look. I get it. You need to share this with me, because you're worried about my reaction. That's sweet of you, but whatever the hell this is, it's about to interrupt my time with you. I'm not stupid, GQ. From the look on your face, you're worried I might decide to end our two-week agreement."

He looked down, his thumb sweeping her knuckles this time. A sense of melancholy hung on him, turning down the corners of his mouth. "I'm not sure I'd blame you if you did."

His voice was a soft, resigned murmur that filled her with dread.

She shook her head. "I don't do this. I decided a long time ago relationships weren't worth it. People leave. Everybody leaves. I'm twenty-five, and I've had one real relationship in my life, and you know what? All it did was prove to me why I don't get involved. It's why I liked that we set a time limit on this. Two weeks, and when that two weeks is up, you go back home and we never see each other again. I leave with my heart intact."

Cade looked up, eyes wide with alarm. "Hannah, after—"

She put a finger to his lips. "I'm done listening, GQ, done talking. For now. Whatever you need to tell me can wait. Our time is limited, and I don't want to ruin it by talking about things that'll steal a piece of that."

Over the last six months, Cade had become a friend, a lover, someone she could talk to and be herself with. For two weeks, he would be hers, and she wanted to enjoy him while she had him. They could get serious later.

She released his hand long enough to take off the overcoat and set it on the bed, then took his hand again and pulled him behind her into the bathroom. There, she took a seat on the edge of the enormous tub and took a moment to start warm water running. Then she turned, hooked Cade by his belt loops, and pulled him toward her. She unbuckled his belt, let her fingers brush his still throbbing erection as she unbuttoned his slacks, and slid down the zipper. She took him in her hand, stroking his length before lifting her gaze to his.

Cade's eyes glittered with heat and amusement. "You're a stubborn little minx, you know that?"

She didn't answer. Instead, she closed her mouth around him, enjoying the feel of him there, the velvet-encased steel. She enjoyed, too, the way, despite his protests, one hand found its way into her hair and fisted. His thighs trembled, the muscles tightening as he braced his legs and rocked his hips forward. He made a sound at the back of his throat, a murmur of a groan that filled her chest with triumph and eased the tension between them.

She flicked her gaze upward, pulled him from her mouth, and licked him like an ice cream cone. "Do you want me to stop, GQ?"

Cade's heavy-lidded eyes blazed back at her. When she took him in her mouth again, his eyes slid shut, his other hand sliding into her hair. "God, no."

She took her time, enjoying giving to him what he'd given to her. It was an intimate act to perform with someone, and the closeness it created made the wall between them evaporate. She needed this connection to him, however small. Here, no complications sat over their heads like a black rain cloud ready to dump on their time together. Things were simple. He was a man, and she was a woman. She gave him pleasure, and he accepted.

She would only admit to herself, though, that his every reaction fed a deep-seated need within, to give, to be accepted, as she was. She wanted to enjoy the intimacy with him, wanted to divest them of the wall that made them, once again, strangers.

She had a sinking feeling she was losing him or would soon. Her time with him seemed finite, in a way it hadn't before his sister's arrival. The thought of going back to a world without him in it made her chest ache. She needed to feel close to him now.

His hands tightened in her hair, the rocking of his hips becoming shaky and jerky. "Hannah…"

His garbled warning came two seconds before he erupted in her mouth with a strangled moan. Hannah took everything he gave.

When the small aftershocks faded, Cade reached down, his hands gripping her shoulders as he pulled her onto her feet and into his arms. He crushed her against his chest and buried his face in the fall of her hair at her shoulder. "God, you're incredible."

She could only cling to him in return. She was definitely in trouble. Her time with him drained like sand in an hourglass; she couldn't stop it. She had one more week left. Eight days. Eight days and she had to give him up. He'd go back to his life. Maybe he'd start seeing other people. The thought of him with someone else made her sick to her stomach.

The thought of losing him, of never again being with him this way, scared her more than a little. She didn't know if she knew how to go back to living the way she had, alone and empty, and she didn't know how to let him go.

* * *

An hour later, they sat together in the tub. Hannah lay with her back to his front, and Cade enjoyed the simple feel of her in his arms. The fingers of one hand ran back and forth along the arm he'd wrapped around her waist, stroking in idle fashion. The other lay on the side of the tub, curled around the stem of her glass of Chardonnay.

They'd been silent for some time. Here, with her in his arms, words never seemed necessary. This time, though, his mind refused to shut off. His gut had tied itself into a thousand knots as he waited for her to give him the okay to tell her his news. He loathed having to tell her, because she was right. It could put an end to their time. She could decide it wasn't what she wanted and walk away from him.

All of which meant that, somewhere over the last two hours, since his sister's unplanned arrival into his relationship with Hannah, the decision weighing on him had made itself. The thought of letting her go, of going back to the way their relationship had been—simple and uncomplicated but shallow—filled him with a hollowness he didn't know how to fill.

Someway, somehow, he had to convince her to give their relationship a chance beyond the physical, beyond these two weeks. He had to convince her he wasn't like the other jerks in her life. That sometimes, taking a chance on something that made no sense could turn out to be the best decision. Even if it only lasted a few months, he had to try. He'd meant what he said. Two weeks wasn't enough time with her. He needed more. He refused to look beyond that or he'd have to admit he was falling for her.

She released a heavy breath and laid her head back against his shoulder. Her voice came as soft as a whisper in the quiet air. "Okay. I'm ready. Tell me."

He drew his own breath, drummed up the courage to say the words he needed to, and prayed he wasn't about to hurt her. "I have an obligation I need to attend."

Her head rocked on his shoulder. "You mentioned that."

So far, so good. "Every year my family attends a local fundraiser for breast cancer research. My father lost several women in his family, and every year we make a sizable donation in their honor."

The fingers on his arm stilled. "What's the catch?"

His gut tightened. Here went nothing.

"This year, they've decided to make the fund-raiser a bachelor auction. Chris runs the committee that sets up the fund-raisers, and last year, the same auction earned over two million in donations. This year, I told her I'd rather donate than participate, but they came up short a couple of bachelors. She volunteered me for the auction block. She also talked Sebastian into attending."

Hannah turned her head. "Sebastian? Is he the one you found with your fiancée?"

"Mmm-hmm. I think Amelia got him drunk and seduced him. I can't help but wonder if Chris volunteered us both for this auction on purpose, as a way to force us together. I have to admit she's right. At some point, I'm going to have to man up and face him, but I'm afraid I don't know how. We each said things we can't take back."

"This auction…the prize is a date with you, right?"

The soft, timid tone of her voice made his chest tighten. It meant Hannah now understood the bigger picture, and he hated the position he had to put her in.

He sighed. There was just no way to make this sound any better.

"Yes. Each bachelor puts together a package the winner receives. Dinner, flowers." He waved a flippant hand in the air, hoping to take the edge off the news. "Women like to be romanced. Chris has taken care of mine. I don't even know what she's drummed up. I only know she's invited some big spenders this year. She's hoping to raise more than they did last year."

Hannah went so still and silent several more knots formed in his gut. Cade held his breath, waiting for her to react, to say something. Silence stretched out between them, and her body tensed against him.

When she wasn't forthcoming, he tightened his hold on her waist and pressed his cheek to hers. "Please say something."

"What's there to say? You have something you need to do. I can't stop you."

The cool aloofness in her tone made his chest tighten. "Hannah…"

She sat forward, pulling away from him. Cool air rushed over his wet skin, leaving goose bumps in her wake. "Besides, the rule was that we couldn't sleep with anyone else. Unless you plan to sleep with her, too, I don't see how this is breaking a rule."

She rose and stepped out of the bath before he could stop her, then pulled a robe from the hook beside the door and left the room.

He swore under his breath and followed after her, yanking a thick white towel from the basket beside the tub and wrapping it around his hips as he went in search of her. He didn't have to go far. He came to a stop outside the bathroom doorway. Hannah sat on the edge of the bed, some ten feet across from him, arms folded across her middle. She stared at the floor, a vacant look in her eye. Her feet dangled several inches over the carpeted floor, swinging back and forth and thumping against the end of the bed.

She might not want to admit it, but he'd done what he'd hoped not to. He'd hurt her, inserted doubt in her mind. He couldn't deny it anymore. She'd become important to him, because the vulnerability written in her expression cut him like a knife.

He crossed the room with careful steps, hoping not to spook her. When she didn't bolt or glare at him, he took a seat beside her and held out his hand, palm up. "You didn't ask me what *I* wanted."

She looked over at him, a challenge glinting in her eyes, but didn't take his hand. "I figured that was obvious. Given that you felt the need to tell me about it means you're going."

He pried one of her hands loose from around her waist and threaded their fingers. Despite that she hadn't voluntarily taken his hand, she didn't pull away, either. The gesture, however small, filled him with hope.

"Several things here. I told you about the auction because I didn't want you hearing it about it secondhand and assuming I was another one of those jerks in your life. The guy who broke your heart did you a favor. You don't need guys like that. I'm not like him, and I never will be. I've been dumped more than once for being too much of a nice guy. I also told you about the auction because I have an idea, but it would require us to break another rule."

She rolled her eyes at him. "You have a thing against rules, don't you?"

He let out a quiet laugh. "No. Actually, I live by them, but this one would get me out of the hot water I find myself in with you. You're upset and I hate I'm the one who put that look on your face. Plus, my idea would solve the problem."

She averted her gaze, looking in the direction of her lap, and lowered her voice. "You're not in hot water with me."

He bumped her shoulder with his. "Then why the long face? Be honest."

She shrugged, but again didn't look at him. "I had a moment of doubt. I don't date for a reason, as I said. I got fed up with always meeting jerks. I seem to find an awful lot of them. When Dane ended it, I gave up."

He nodded. "And you wondered if I was another one."

"No. I wondered if maybe you were telling me you'd had enough of me. I wondered…" She shook her head. "Never mind."

He hated that she had the thought, hated he knew what it was like to doubt your own worth, to doubt whether or not you'd ever find someone who saw *you*. Hated she still didn't seem to believe he wanted *her*. Of all the women he could have ended up with, he couldn't be more grateful that he'd ended up with Hannah.

He looked over at her, staring at her profile. He shouldn't say it. The warning filled his brain, bright, flashing neon that all said, *Don't say it!* Giving voice to the words seated on the tip of his tongue would be crossing a line. A big one.

The words left his mouth anyway, on a need to somehow prove to her he wasn't one of those jerks. Whatever their relationship had started as, he'd hate himself if he ever hurt her the way the others in her life had. "You want to know what I'm thinking right now?"

She laughed, a quiet, dismissive huff. "No. Not really."

He leaned over, bending his mouth to her ear. Her soft scent, the oils she'd put in the bath water, swirled around him. He ached to bite her earlobe, to nibble his way up her neck until she melted into him and let out that quiet, addicting little moan. "I think you're beautiful the way you are. When I'm with you, I relax. In a way I can't seem to do on my own. Baby, I even sleep better with you, and you bring out a playfulness in me. We laugh together. A lot. And I'm addicted to it. Two weeks isn't enough time with you. I want more."

Her gaze snapped to his. Her breathing grew rapid and shallow, and she stared at him, wide-eyed, like he'd just told her he'd murdered three people.

She surged to her feet in a flurry of sudden movement. She stripped her robe, dropping it to the floor behind her, then snatched her tan overcoat off the end of the bed, putting it on as she made a beeline for the exit.

"Two weeks, Cade. We agreed on two weeks, no more, no less, no strings attached. You don't get to change the rules on a whim because you feel like it." She strode from the room, her soft, bare footsteps fading through the suite. Seconds later, the door to the suite slammed shut.

Cade blew out a defeated breath. He ached to go after her, but experience with his sister told him Hannah needed time to cool off. He knew he'd changed the rules, but he had to take this chance. He had no idea if their relationship would even survive. Maybe it would fail. Maybe it would burn out in a few months.

He still had to take the chance. When he'd ended it with Amelia, he was positive he would never meet a single woman who'd accept him at face value, who wouldn't use him for what she could gain from an alignment with his family.

Until Hannah. She was the first woman in a long time who made him believe in possibilities. That maybe women *weren't* all the same. Maybe there were women out there who wanted the same things he did—someone honest with whom to fill the empty spaces. He was an old-fashioned kind of guy. He couldn't deny it. He wanted someone to spend his life with, someone to curl around at the end of the day.

He hadn't a clue if that was Hannah, but he had to find out. More than anything, he needed to prove to her not all men were like those self-serving jerks she'd managed to find. Hannah deserved to know she was beautiful—and worth the effort—the way she was.

All of which meant he couldn't give her up without a fight. As he sat there, plans began to fill his mind. He was going to sweep one Hannah Miller clean off her feet, and he knew exactly where to start.

Chapter Nine

Hannah pulled open her apartment door and froze. Once again, Cade stood out in the hallway, reminiscent of the night he'd shown up in his pajamas. This time, however, he wore a suit. A crisp, light blue shirt, a dark blue tie, and navy slacks topped by a navy jacket. She loved him in a suit. The ensemble fit him to perfection and made her heart beat a little faster.

He also wore glasses, the kind with no frames that all but disappeared on his face. Somehow, they made him appear smarter. Intellectual.

What he held in his hand, however, gained her full attention. Her red stilettos dangled from his left hand, and over his left arm lay a black garment bag.

"I didn't know you wore glasses." As the words left her mouth, Hannah immediately regretted them. What a stupid thing to say. Except she didn't know what else *to* say. He'd been calling and texting several times a day since she'd left him in his hotel room two days before. She hated avoiding him, but she didn't know how to face him, either. He wanted things she couldn't give him, because sooner or later, their relationship would end. He was from a different world, and one day, he'd wake up and realize he didn't want her.

He reached up to touch the edge of the frames and nodded absently.

"Forgot I had them on. I've been in meetings all day. I need them mostly to read, but I've gotten so used to them I sometimes forget they're there." He stuck a hand in his right pocket, pulled out his fist, then turned it over and opened it. In his palm sat the red lace panties she'd left at his hotel, now carefully folded. "You haven't returned my calls. I figured you might like these back."

She ought to apologize, at the very least for the way she'd left, but she wasn't sorry. She had boundaries she needed to reset. He'd gotten far too important and she had to put a stop to it now. Cade McKenzie was supposed to be a toy, a sexy little fling with a definite ending date. No more, no less, and no damn strings. She liked it that way. Preferred it that way.

The thought of setting her heart in someone else's hands terrified her. She'd spent her life keeping people at a distance. It was easier than getting attached to someone who'd leave in the end. She'd learned the lesson the hard way growing up in the home. Her life had been a series of relationships ending in heartbreak. Kids she'd befriended left the group home, never to be seen or heard from again. Families she'd lived with eventually sent her back, and when she turned eighteen, she aged out of the system and she was let go.

The few times she'd tried to have something more than fleeting had turned out disastrously, proving she didn't need anybody but herself. How Maddie ended up under her radar she had no idea. It was a pathetic way to live, but it served its purpose over the years.

"Thank you." Her face heated a million degrees as she reached out to take her panties from his palm. She'd been so upset when she'd left his hotel, she'd marched back to the store wearing nothing but Maddie's tan overcoat. She hadn't even realized she'd forgotten her meager clothing until Maddie pointed out her bare feet and asked where her heels had gone.

Apparently, Cade intended to torment her some more, for he reached into the left inside pocket of his jacket and pulled out the cupless bra that went with her ensemble. One corner of his mouth quirked upward as he held it out to her, dangling off the end of his index finger. "And this."

She darted a nervous glance out into the hallway behind him. God, if one of her neighbors walked by…Luckily for her, the hallway was deserted.

She snatched the bra from his finger. His mouth twitched, eyes glittering in triumph.

Next he held out the shoes.

"These you're going to need." When she took the shoes from him, he picked up the garment bag and held it out to her as well. "They go well with this."

She stared at the bag for a moment, then met his gaze again and shook her head in confusion. "What is it?"

He shook the bag, and she accepted but didn't open the zipper.

"It's a dress. Handpicked. Chris helped me guess your size. She assures me it'll look fabulous on you." Cade reached into his left front pocket again, this time pulling out an envelope and held it out to her. "You're going to need them to go with this. It's an invitation. The auction is tomorrow at six. That's the part you didn't let me finish. I can't refuse this auction. It's a worthy cause, and it's too late to find another bachelor to take my place. Should you decide to accept, Chris's number is on the invitation. She said to tell you she'll take care of everything. You just have to show up."

Hannah drew her brows together and shook her head. "I don't understand."

He took the garment bag from her hand, set the hanger on the doorknob, and hooked her around the waist, tugging her flush against his length.

Hannah's breath caught in her throat. The full press of his body was more sensation than she could handle. The warm, solid press of all those muscles made her forget her name. The scent of his cologne went to her head in a dizzying rush. The determined look in his eye made her weak in the knees. Cade was large and in control, and everything inside of her trembled beneath the power of him.

His fingers caressed her back where he held her close. "I'd like you to attend the auction. I want you to bid. On me. They'll be handing out bidding numbers. All you have to do is raise yours and make sure nobody outbids you. Chris will take care of the funds."

So, that's what this is all about. God, he had no idea what he did to her. How much she yearned to go to the auction and stake her claim on him. Which was why she wouldn't.

Hannah pushed out of his arms, left the garment bag hanging on the door, and turned, moving into the living room to lay her belongings on the couch. "I think maybe it's best if you *do* go out with someone else. It's why I left the hotel the other day. I can't give you what you want. This is more than we agreed on. I'm sorry, but I can't do this anymore."

Cade remained silent behind her for a long, unnerving minute. Hands braced on the back of the couch, she couldn't bring herself to turn and face him. She hated the thought of ending their time together, but he asked for more than she could give.

Behind her, the door closed with a soft snap. Moments later, he laid the garment bag over the back of the couch beside her, and his warmth filled her back. "I'm a patient man, and I have all the time in the world. I'm willing to wait you out, but I'm not giving up."

For a moment, Hannah couldn't breathe. She stiffened, a vague, pathetic attempt to put some last-ditch space between them. "I believe that's called stalking."

He had the audacity to laugh, light and amused; then he leaned into her. His entire length pressed into her, from his firm, broad chest against her back down to his lean hips against her ass. His erection pressed into the cleft between her cheeks. His warm breath feathered over her neck. His lips moved against the delicate skin of her earlobe as he leaned into her.

"Can you deny you want the same thing? Isn't that why you left? Because the thought of me with someone else makes you crazy? I think you want more, too, but you're terrified I'm another jerk."

Hannah closed her eyes and bit her lower lip, her nails digging into the couch cushion. Damn the man. He knew how to get to her, knew every button to push, because she'd told him, in intimate detail.

"You should also know, baby, I'm a determined man, and I'm used to getting what I want. It makes me *very* good at my job. And in case there's any doubt, what I want is you." His lips skimmed her shoulder and up her neck. The tender caress lit every inch of her on fire. He ended the torture by flicking his tongue against her earlobe. His breath blew hot against her neck. "*Only* you."

Cade released her and stepped back. Several moments of silence passed. The quiet echo of his footsteps over the wooden floorboards provided the only sound in the otherwise dead silent apartment, followed by the creak of her front door opening. She couldn't bring herself to turn or she'd be in his arms. Her whole body trembled with the desperate need to close her mouth over his and lose herself in his drugging kisses.

He had her eating out of the palm of his hand, and she didn't even have the strength to deny it.

"Oh, and bring Maddie. I'm going to be busy during the auction, and she'll give you someone to hang out with. Something tells me she'll enjoy this. Afterward, I have plans for you. Well, us really, but it's all for you."

The door closed with a quiet snap. Hannah managed to turn but couldn't do much more than stare, openmouthed, in his wake. Why did she get the feeling of being a fish in a barrel? Cade McKenzie had staked his claim on her, and she couldn't even draw enough breath to deny him.

* * *

The next morning, she was in the shop by nine. She hadn't slept a wink last night. She'd spent the night tossing and turning, pondering the things Cade had told her. By the time eight o'clock came, she gave up attempting to sleep. She needed to talk to her best friend. Maddie, thank goodness, was always the first one in the shop. She stood behind the counter. What looked like inventory sheets sat in front of her. As Hannah breezed in, she looked up.

One look at her, and Maddie abandoned the papers, her eyes wide with alarm. "You look like you've seen a ghost. What's wrong? What happened?"

Hannah shook her head as she plopped, unladylike, onto the stool behind the counter. "I'm in so much trouble, Madds."

Maddie's fiery brows drew together, her hands already on her hips. "He hasn't become one of those jerks, has he?"

Hannah sighed, shoulders slumping. "Quite the opposite. He's intelligent, articulate, and playful. He's a nice guy. He reads for crying out loud, and I feel good when I'm with him."

Maddie laughed. "And how is this a bad thing?"

Hannah threw her hands in the air in exasperation and shook her head.

"Two weeks, Madds. We agreed on two weeks, no strings attached." She dropped her hands and sighed. "Cade wants more."

Maddie's brows shot up into her hair. "*More?*"

Hannah nodded. "More. He came over last night to invite me to an auction. It's tonight, at six. I haven't decided whether or not I'm going."

"Ah." Maddie nodded, a knowing light in her eyes. "Because if you go, you'll be admitting you want more, too. What's the auction for?"

Hannah sighed. "It's for breast cancer research. It's a bachelor auction, and he's one of the bachelors. His sister, twin sister, by the way, signed him up and dropped it on him last minute. He wants me to go and bid on him."

Maddie shook her head.

"I'm not seeing the down side here, sweetie. Enjoy the hell out of him." She flashed a wicked grin and winked. "Hell, enjoy him once for me, would you? And find out if he's got a brother."

Hannah smiled in spite of herself, but the nagging heaviness wouldn't leave her chest. "I have rules, Madds. I've always had rules. Don't get attached, because people always leave. A man like him, from a world like his? Why would he want someone like me? He's out of my league. So far out of my league it's almost humorous. At some point, he's going to realize it, and it's going to end."

Maddie pursed her lips, brow furrowed in disapproval, and shook her head. "I'm going to save you the 'how wrong you are' speech, since I know you've heard it before. I *will* say this. So what if it ends? At least this time it's *your* choice, with a guy who's crazy about you. Look, I get it. This isn't easy for you. I know that even having this fling with him is so far out of the box you might as well be on the moon. But you have to ask yourself something, sweetie. When it's all said and done, what will you regret more? Doing it? Or being too afraid to take the chance? You like him, right? Be honest."

Hannah let her shoulders slump. She couldn't deny it. "Yes."

Maddie wrapped an arm around her shoulders and hugged her tight.

"Then go for it, follow wherever it leads. Have a fling you'll look back on in ten years and smile about. As long as he's not a jerk, enjoy him while you've got him, however long it is, whether it's two weeks, two months, or two years." Maddie's bright, positive expression fell. "Because trust me, you'll regret not taking the chance."

Melancholy crept into Maddie's voice, and Hannah couldn't help but smile. "Speaking from experience?"

Maddie's back stiffened. She folded her arms, jutting her chin at a stubborn angle.

Hannah cocked her head. "Admit it. You regret not sleeping with Grayson."

Maddie let out a derisive snort. "Hardly. I regret a lot of things about him, but not sleeping with him is most definitely not one of them."

Hannah nudged her with an elbow. "Methinks the lady doth protest too much."

Maddie rolled her eyes. "Grayson Lockwood turned out to be a pompous ass, and I'm grateful I wasn't stupid enough to fall for his charms."

Hannah pursed her lips and furrowed her brow. "No, you're not. Give it up. If you could do it again, would you?"

"All right. The man is sexy as sin. The pompous ass makes my knees weak and my panties damp. He's sex on legs. He knows it, too. Damn him." Maddie darted a narrowed glance in her direction, but one corner of her mouth lifted, betraying her. "There. You satisfied?"

Hannah couldn't resist a grin. "Yes, thank you, but would you?"

"Honestly? I don't know. He lied to me, and I can't ignore

that. He could very easily have told me the truth. But would I do it differently if I could?" Maddie heaved a sigh, her shoulders rounding, and waved her hand in the air. "I don't know. Maybe if I could tape his mouth shut. He could just…lie there and look pretty."

Hannah giggled.

Maddie's gaze snapped to hers, her brow furrowed in determination. She jabbed a pointed finger in Hannah's direction. "Which is why you're going to the auction. Girl, the man made a point to tell you where he'd be. He gave you an invitation and set up everything, including how you're going to pay the several millions dollars women are going to be bidding on him. And they will, because, honey, he is *fine*, with a capital *F*. Women will be clamoring to get at him, drooling over his luscious self."

Hannah glared at her best friend. "Would you stop?"

Maddie cocked a brow. "I'm serious. Do you really want to stay at home, in your self-imposed shell of isolation, knowing he's out with someone else? Even if he doesn't sleep with her, even if it's only an obligation date, do you want to give him the chance?"

Hannah averted her gaze, peering out the front window, and sighed. "I hate the thought of him with someone else. It makes me want to claw her eyes out, whoever it is he ends up with. Or climb on top of him and proclaim him all mine."

Maddie gave a decisive nod. "Exactly. So, you're going."

Hannah surged off the stool, pacing the length of the counter and back again. Her mind ran in circles, but the third time back to her stool, the decision made itself. She couldn't deny it. Maddie was right. She had to go or Cade would end up on a date with another woman, and she couldn't let it happen. She simply couldn't.

If this happened, though, it would be on *her* terms.

Decision made, she halted and turned. "Fine, but you're coming with me. I will *not* go into the lion's den and face those women alone."

The instant the words left her mouth, Hannah regretted her harsh tone, but Maddie, true to her usual self, didn't bat an eyelash. Rather, she winked, her grin playful and mischievous.

"Hunky single men in tuxes are being auctioned off, for charity no less. Honey, I wouldn't miss this for the world." Maddie looped an arm around her shoulders. "Don't you worry, sweets. We're going to have a blast!"

* * *

By the time they arrived that night, Hannah's heart had taken a firm place in her throat. She couldn't seem to stop shaking. They held the auction on the fourth floor of a local hotel, in one of the grand ballrooms. The space had a calm elegance to it. Everything, from the soft carpeting beneath her feet to the draperies lining the walls, had been done in shades of blue. On the far end stood a small stage, containing a podium with a microphone. Hundreds of black chairs lined the floor in front, with an aisle running down the center.

Standing inside the entrance, Hannah scanned the room for any sign of Cade or Christina. People, the majority of them women, packed the small square room, spilling between the chairs surrounding the tiny stage and the bar off to the right.

Every one of them was dressed to the nines. To top it off, waitresses moved through the crowd with trays of champagne flutes, and a small dance floor had been segregated on the left.

Hannah smoothed a shaking palm down the skirt of her dress, overwhelmed by the sight before her. She had the sudden sensation of being a square in a room full of circles. The dress Cade had given her was beautiful. It had a keyhole halter neckline, a pleated empire waist, and a tiered skirt ending in a layered handkerchief hem. She had to admit the way the wispy fabric swished around her thighs made her feel beautiful but like a complete phony. She didn't fit in with these people.

She turned her head, scanning the room. These women all carried themselves with an air of elegance and sophistication Hannah couldn't match. Looking at them all, her mind filled with questions. Which one would counterbid on Cade? Would it be the tall, leggy blonde by the bar? Or the curvy brunette in front of the stage?

Her stomach churned. She grabbed Maddie's elbow, panic clawing at her throat. "I can't do this, Madds. I don't fit in with these women. Look at them. They're all so regal and elegant in their long gowns and expensive jewels. They even *look* rich. I can't compete with them."

Maddie caught her hand, pulled her away from the entrance, and turned to her, gripping her hands tightly. Maddie herself wore a simple but elegant black sheath dress. It accentuated her fantastic curves.

"Yes, you can and you will, because if you don't, your man will be spending the evening with one of them. Sweetie, you might not think so, but you look phenomenal in that dress. Your man has a fantastic eye, because that dress floats over you and hides everything you always say you hate about your body." She turned and nodded off to the right. "See that guy over there? The blond by the bar? He's been staring at you since we walked in. *You*, sweetheart, not me."

Hannah followed Maddie's gaze. The man in question caught her eye, tipped his head, and smiled. Hannah flushed to the roots of her hair and averted her gaze to the floor. Men didn't look at her with such blatant admiration in their gazes. Obviously, he couldn't see her scar from this angle.

Maddie squeezed her hand. "Hold your head up high, sweets. You look phenomenal."

"Oh my goodness, you're here!"

Hannah followed the familiar feminine voice. Off to her left, Christina strode in their direction, her face lit with an excited smile. She looked incredible. Her little black dress hugged and accentuated her every flawless curve, classic but stunning. Beside her, a tall dark-haired gentleman in a black tux kept pace with her, his gate long and lanky.

Christina ran the last few steps like an excited child and enveloped her in an overwhelming hug, squeezing so tight for a moment, Hannah's breath caught. "I'm so glad you guys could come."

The dark-haired gentleman chuckled. He caught Hannah's stunned gaze.

"You get used to her after a while. Our Tina is a hugger." He extended a hand. "Sebastian Blake. Bachelor number eleven." He winked and tapped the nametag on his chest.

Hannah smiled and shook his hand. "Nice to meet you."

Intrigued by another aspect of Cade's life, Hannah couldn't help taking him in. Sebastian reminded her a lot of Cade. Well over six feet tall, broad shoulders and a wide chest that filled out his fitted tux to perfection. His hair was lighter, though, more of a dark brown, his eyes a beautiful shade of deep blue. Where Cade always seemed quiet and intense, Sebastian had a playful air about him.

Beside him, a look somewhere between petulance and irritation moved across Christina's features. "Forgive him. He's determined to make me pay for the fact that I volunteered him."

Sebastian narrowed his eyes, but the corners of his mouth twitched. "Without bothering to ask, no less."

"Oh, please, I knew darn well you wouldn't have anything else to do this evening and it's for a good cause. You had a blast last year." Christina shook her head, frowning in disapproval. "Baz here likes to be the center of attention. He ended up doing a mock strip tease last year. Stripped all the way down to his bare chest. The women loved it."

Sebastian winked, a proud sparkle in his eye. "Got me the highest bid of the night."

Maddie nudged her with an elbow, and Hannah let out a nervous laugh. She'd done it again, gotten so caught up in Cade she'd forgotten her best friend.

"Oh, I'm so sorry. I'm so nervous. Christina, this is my friend and business partner, Madison O'Riley." She glanced beside her and extended a hand in introduction toward Christina. "Maddie, this is Cade's sister, Christina."

"So nice to meet you." Maddie turned her head from side to

side, looking around her as she shook Christina's hand. "It's quite the shindig you've set up here. Looks like fun."

Christina beamed, this one bright and genuine.

"Oh, they're always so much fun. Last year we had a ball. A bunch of women getting together to outbid each other over gorgeous men…We girls can get a little rowdy." Christina let out a breathy laugh, then turned to Hannah, brow raised in silent question. "Has Caden found you yet?"

Hannah shook her head. "We just arrived." She looked around her for a moment, taking in the room, then swallowed past the lump of fear stuck in her throat. "I have to admit I'm nervous. I've never done this before."

Christina stepped forward, wrapping her in another hug.

"Don't be. It's a piece of cake." She leaned back, holding Hannah by the upper arms as she looked her over from head to toe. "Oh, I knew that dress would fit to perfection. You look wonderful."

When Christina's gaze shifted to something behind her and Sebastian stiffened, his mouth forming a thin line, Hannah knew on instinct Cade had stepped up behind her.

Christina confirmed the thought when her expression lit up. "Caden, there you are. I told you she'd look fabulous in this dress."

"She's right. You look incredible."

The husky rumble of his voice had goose bumps popping up along the surface of her skin. Every nerve ending vibrated with acute awareness of his presence behind her, and every fiber of her being begged her to turn and throw herself into his arms. She'd only admit it to herself, but she'd missed him.

Instead, she drew up straight, attempting to prepare herself for the addicting sight of him. Somehow, she had to face him and not melt into a puddle at his feet. She had to keep him from ending up with someone else tonight, while also convincing him their two weeks was what she wanted, and she had to do it all without bowing beneath the force of his seductive presence.

If she made it through this night with her sanity and her heart intact, it would be a miracle.

* * *

As he stepped into the small circle of people, Cade focused his attention on Hannah and the vision she made. Her dress caressed her curves, accentuating every blessed one. She'd even worn her hair up off her face, in a neat twist at the back of her head. She looked incredible and he had to admit, he was smitten.

Right then, he wanted more than anything to be alone with her. He ached to hike up the hem of her dress and bury himself so damn deep inside of her he couldn't tell where he ended and she began. Until he forgot everything but the sweet lavender scent of her skin and the addicting way she clung to him right before her orgasm ripped through her.

He didn't want to be at this damn auction. He didn't want to stand in a circle of people he ought to feel comfortable with and somehow still feel like a stranger. Sebastian's cool aloof stare drove him nuts. Too much water flowed under that particular bridge and he hadn't the foggiest damn idea how to fix it.

Hannah's gaze flicked to him, and he let the lull of it pull him in. Wariness still hovered in her eyes. She seemed determined to keep him at arm's length. To top it off, not being able to touch her killed him. Their time ticked out like the final seconds of a football game, with no way to stop the clock, and every second he spent without her felt flat-out wrong.

He couldn't ignore, however, that she'd come. That alone said something huge. It was a tiny step, but one in the right direction. He'd take what he could get.

He tossed her a smile and, unable to resist, touched her arm.

"I'm glad you could make it." He shifted his gaze to Maddie beside her. "Nice to see you again, Miss O'Riley. You clean up rather nicely."

She arched a brow, a teasing gleam in her eyes. "You don't look so bad yourself there, hot stuff."

She had the audacity to wink at him, and Cade couldn't help but laugh. Whoever she ended up with would no doubt have his hands full.

Maddie touched Hannah's elbow. "I'll leave you to chat and go grab us a couple glasses of champagne."

Sebastian stiffened and nodded politely in Hannah's direction. "It was nice to meet you. I think I'll join your friend for that drink."

Sebastian turned away, but Chris caught his sleeve, stopping his retreat before he managed to get more than a single stride away. She furrowed her brow. "Oh, for crying out loud. The two of you are acting like children."

Whatever playfulness had been between them before evaporated with the icy glare Sebastian shot Chris. The muscle in his jaw jumped. "Leave it alone, Tina."

Tina. Sebastian was the only person who called her that. It was a childhood nickname that had stuck, and Chris hated it.

True to her nature, Chris didn't bat an eyelash. She planted her hands on her hips and glared right back. "You've been friends for over twenty years. Are you really going to let it end this way? Over someone like *her*?"

"I'm the one who got hit, remember?" Sebastian threw a glare in Cade's direction, then pivoted and stalked off.

Chris stormed after him, catching him some twenty feet beyond them. She planted her hands on her hips. He couldn't hear their conversation, but if he knew his sister, she was lecturing the poor bastard, for she glared right back at him and jabbed a finger in their direction.

Sebastian, never one to be intimidated by anyone, least of all Chris, matched her expression, his dark brows furrowed. When Chris didn't back down but poked him in the chest, he bent down, getting in her face. Her expression shifted, her jaw tightening, but tears twinkled in the low light of the room. She hiked her chin a notch, pivoted, and marched in the opposite direction. Sebastian dragged frustrated hands through his hair.

Cade released a heavy breath. "She shouldn't pick fights with him. He won't admit it, but it wounds him."

"Sebastian has a crush on her, doesn't he?"

Cade laughed and shook his head. "Oh, it's more than a crush. He's been head over heels for her since somewhere around college. I think there's a high chance it's mutual."

"That doesn't bother you?"

Cade shrugged. "It used to. Sebastian doesn't do commitment and never has. He's always played the part of the playboy. He goes through women like there's an endless supply, and he's determined none of them will ever tie him down. But deep down where it counts, I'd trust him with her life. I can't ignore that."

Hannah touched his shoulder, her hand warm and alluring. "You know, apologies go a long way. Even if you aren't wrong, it often soothes the wound."

Cade shook his head and sighed.

"I've apologized. More than once. He hasn't decided to forgive me yet. I'm afraid there's too much water under that bridge. He's right. I hit him. It was a knee-jerk reaction, and it ended in us yelling things at each other. He and I both said things we can't take back." He released the pent-up regret seated in his stomach and turned his head, finally meeting her gaze. "I'm glad you came. Does this mean what I hope it does?"

Hannah studied him for a moment, eyes anxious and darting over his face. Finally, she pulled her shoulders back. "I want what we agreed on. Two weeks. No more, no less."

He studied her for a long moment. There were two ways he could play this. He could continue to try being patient, or he could stop being polite and stake his claim. Right now, he needed her to be straight with him. Whatever it meant. Conflict warred with the fear dancing in the depths of her eyes, telling him she held her cards close to her chest. If it were the last thing he did, he'd break through her walls.

Deciding to call her bluff, he arched a brow. "The pulse at the base of your neck gives you away, baby. So does your breathing. Your chest is rising and falling at a rapid pace, and your eyes are everywhere but on me."

Her breathing ramped up another notch. When he took a step toward her, she took a step back.

Cade caught her around the waist, stopping her retreat, and leaned his head beside her ear. "Tell me something, baby. How damp are your panties right now?"

He forced himself to pull back enough to see her face—because if he didn't, his mouth would attach itself to hers, right there in front of everyone.

Heat flared in the depths of her eyes, but her chin jutted at a defiant angle. "Who says I'm wearing any?"

Those words from her mouth were his breaking point. In two seconds flat, she had him imagining her bare bottom beneath her dress. It would be so easy to hike up the hem and sink into her velvet heat. He'd spent three days without her.

His cock hardened behind his fly. He picked up her hand and pivoted, tugging her behind him as he strode from the ballroom in search of a space, any space, where a hundred pairs of eyes weren't watching his every damn move. He moved out of the ballroom into the hallway beyond; his gaze landed on the stairwell doorway at the end, and he turned toward it.

Halfway down the hallway, Hannah tugged on his arm. "Cade. Heels and short legs. Please slow down."

He slowed his pace a fraction but didn't stop. He didn't trust himself. If he stopped, he'd be fucking her against the nearest wall. His balls ached with the desperate need to bury himself to the hilt in her slippery heat. He wanted to be as close to her as humanly possible, to convince her he wasn't the enemy. He needed the connection to her like he needed to draw his next breath. It had him shaking.

He hit the door leading to the stairwell at full stride. Once out beyond the crowd of people, the silence of the space washed over him. The door clicked shut, the thud echoing up the stairwell.

He leaned over the railing, checking to be sure they were alone, then turned and pressed her back against the wall. His hands had a mind of their own, wandering over her curves as he trailed his lips over the exposed skin of her neck and shoulders. He sucked, licked, and nibbled his way across the hard line of her stubborn jaw and down the supple softness of her neck. It didn't escape his notice that she didn't protest but melted against him.

"You shouldn't tease me right now, baby. I haven't seen you in three days." He pressed his aching cock into the softness of her belly. All the while the words pent up in his chest kept leaving his mouth, on a desperate need to convince her following their hearts was a good thing. "Feel that? That's what you do to me. All I have to do is think about you and my body rises to yours. Christ, the way I need you scares the hell out of me."

"Cade, please…" Despite her plea, her hips pushed back, rocking against him, and her hands closed around the lapels of his jacket.

Too afraid he really would hike her dress around her waist and take her right there, Cade forced himself to release her enough to meet her gaze. "If that's the way you felt, why did you even come tonight?"

The seconds ticked out as he waited. Hannah stared at him, wide-eyed and stunned. Her chest rose and fell at an increased pace.

From out in the hallway, an announcement came over the speakers in the ballroom down the hall, a dull hum from this distance, but he knew what it meant.

So did Hannah, for she turned away from him, stepping sideways to slip past him. "They're starting. We need to get back."

Cade set his hand on the wall beside her side head, stopping her retreat before she'd gotten more than a step away. He had one chance at this. He wouldn't ruin it by holding back now.

He leaned his mouth to her ear. "This might have started out as a fling, baby, but I want more, and I think you do, too. I think that's what scares you so much. I'm not giving up on you, because I think you expect me to. I'm not like those other jerks in your life, and I *will* prove it."

Having no desire to hear her rebuttal, he turned and left the stairwell. He had every intention of laying his heart on the line but this wasn't the time or the place. If only she'd hold on long enough to see him through this damn obligation.

Chapter Ten

Hannah exited the stairwell and made a beeline for the bathroom, not stopping until she had her hands on the cool tile of the sink's edge. She drew in deep gulping breaths and stared at her reflection in the mirror, attempting to calm the fierce pounding of her heart. Coming to this auction had been a bad idea. Cade was right. He terrified her, and letting him have this date would give her a reason to end the insanity waging a war in her head.

Cade had staked his claim. His words and the dark expression on his face had said that loud and clear. She had to admit his speech had threatened to melt her right out of her dress.

Long distance never worked. Eventually, he'd grow tired of her. They all did. She couldn't wait around for the time to come, for her heart to get broken. So why stay?

Because the thought of him with someone else made her chest tighten to painful proportions. She sighed, dropped her head, and closed her eyes. She might only have six days left with him, but she wanted every single one.

The bathroom door creaked open, interrupting her train of thought, and Hannah opened her eyes. A tall, very pregnant blonde sashayed in. In an ankle-length gown that caressed the expanse of her stomach, the woman strode to the sinks with a confident stride, her low heels clicking soundly on the coffee-colored floor tiles. As she stepped up to the sink, her gaze flicked over Hannah, her mouth pursing in disapproval before she turned to her reflection.

The woman pulled lip gloss out of her small clutch purse. "He'll never be yours, you know."

Hannah froze, watching the other woman in the mirror. "I'm sorry, do I know you?"

The blonde didn't even have the courage to turn and meet her gaze but ran a hand over her stomach and turned sideways in order to lean toward the mirror instead. She dabbed the tip of her fourth finger into the gloss, then smoothed it across full, plump lips.

"My name is Amelia Prescott. Seven months ago, I was you. This baby? Is Caden's. A word of warning, honey. Caden McKenzie will never marry a woman outside his own class. You can put on a pretty dress and expensive-looking shoes, but you'll never be one of them. You're a toy to him, something to fill his time while he's here on business."

An eerie chill ran the length of her spine. Cade's ex, and she was pregnant. The thought had every uncertainty rising like a typhoon over her head and filled her with questions. Cade hadn't mentioned this aspect of his relationship with his ex. Was the baby really his? Or was this all an act for her benefit?

Determined not to let the woman unseat her, Hannah let out

a scoffing laugh and began washing her hands for something innocuous to do. "And I should believe you why? The way I heard it, you slept with his best friend."

Amelia straightened away from the sink, irritation forming deep grooves between her brows. "Look, I'm trying to save you the heartache, because you seem like a nice girl. You're right. I screwed up, and I slept with Sebastian. I told Cade I was pregnant and he denied it. Go ahead. Ask him. I was hurt and I did something stupid for revenge. Tell me you've never made a mistake you wished you could take back?"

Hannah laughed. "Not that kind of mistake, no. *I* have a sense of morality."

Amelia drew up straight, her expression one of instant disapproval. "You can hate me all you want, sweetheart, but the cold truth is Caden McKenzie plays with girls like you and me. He doesn't marry them. Did he tell you he has a son?"

"Yes, he did." Hannah moved to the paper towel dispenser, yanked out two, and dried her hands as fast as she could. She wanted out of this bathroom and away from this nutcase.

"Did he tell you he gave the baby up for adoption?" Amelia stuffed her lip gloss back into her clutch and touched a hand to her oversprayed hairdo. "His girlfriend at the time was a girl like you and me, from the wrong side of the tracks. A nobody his parents didn't approve of. I'd hasten to guess you haven't met the parents yet? I've known Caden since primary school. My family's not part of their world either. My father worked two jobs to put me through private school, but his mother didn't approve. Do you see the pattern, sweetie? Get out while you can."

Amelia tucked her purse in the crook of her arm and strode from the room with a swirl of skirts.

When the bathroom door fell shut again, Hannah turned and sagged back against the cool tile wall. She dragged in gulping breaths in an effort to quell the panic rising behind her breastbone. She couldn't deny it anymore. The truth stared her in the face like a blinking neon sign. Amelia might be a self-righteous bitch with an underhanded motive, but even Hannah couldn't deny the truth of what she'd said. She and Cade were from two different worlds, and she didn't fit into his. Nothing had proven that to her more than being here, at this stupid auction. She felt out of place amidst all these rich women and over her head.

Sooner or later, Cade would get bored with her. They all did, including Dane, who'd sworn when they started dating she was the kind of woman he wanted. The question was, how much of her heart would be left when Cade came to his senses and realized she wasn't what he wanted either?

By the time she returned to the ballroom, she was shaking. The beginnings of panic clawed its way up her limbs to her throat, and her knees wobbled as she made her way to her seat. When she plopped down with a little less finesse than intended, Maddie glanced at her.

Brow furrowed, Maddie leaned toward her, whispering, "You okay? You're a little pale."

Hannah closed her eyes and drew in a deep breath in an attempt to calm her trembling nerves. She had to make the best of this. Damned if she'd let Amelia's cruel words get to her, to allow one more person's lack of humanity crush her spirit.

A bit calmer, she opened her eyes and leaned toward Maddie,

whispering back, "His ex cornered me in the bathroom. I think she tried to intimidate me."

Maddie's eyes narrowed to thin slits, her mouth forming a thin line. "Oooh, honey, you can't let her win."

Hannah sat straighter in her seat, her bid number clutched tightly in her hand. She swallowed past the rising fear. "I don't intend to."

Waiting for Cade's turn to creep up, however, took forever. Over an hour passed before they moved through the first ten bachelors. They seemed to be saving the best for last, for each bachelor got a higher and higher bid. Sebastian's turn came eleventh in line and one before Cade. By the time he took his place beside Christina and the auctioneer at the podium, Hannah's stomach had tied itself into sickening knots.

Christina stepped up to the microphone, her smile bright and gracious. "All right, ladies, our next bachelor is someone I've known for most of my life. Sebastian Blake is thirty-one. He has a cat named Spike—."

Someone meowed, and Christina lost track of her sentence, her smile faltering as she looked out at the audience again. Hurt flashed in the depths of her eyes, there and gone as Christina flashed a bright smile. "I see we have cat lovers among us tonight."

Laughter rolled through the audience, and Christina looked back to her note cards.

"His favorite ice cream flavor is rocky road. He plays the guitar..." She glanced up at this and winked. "And well, I might add. He also works out religiously."

A loud, appreciative whistle pierced the room from somewhere in the audience behind Hannah. Sebastian grinned, made a show of taking off his jacket and cocked an arm, flexing one beefy bicep. Several enthusiastic whoops came from the back of the room.

The same woman who, three days ago, barged into her brother's hotel room faltered. Christina's expression fell. She went silent, staring at something in the back of the room. After a long, awkward moment, she let out a laugh that to Hannah's ears sounded forced, and shook her head.

"Always the class clown, Baz." She winked. "Ladies, it's never a dull moment with this one. You're sure to have a great time. Sebastian is the CEO of Blake Hotels and Resorts, which means that in addition to an evening with him, the package also includes a weekend of being pampered."

As the auctioneer started the bidding, three women put in bids, each one higher than the last. One woman, a tall blonde in her forties, ended the war by making an outrageous bid of two million dollars.

As Sebastian exited the stage to greet and no doubt thank the winner, Christina's bright expression fell. Something flashed in her gaze. It was there and gone in the blink of an eye. A deep breath later, she squared her shoulders and put on another easy smile, clapping and congratulating the woman who'd won. Hannah had felt the emotion enough times to recognize it in someone else: hurt. Hannah's heart went out to her. Christina looked about how Hannah felt right then, like she was on the verge of losing something, or in this case, some*one*, important to her.

Hannah's heart sank into her toes. She shifted her gaze to Cade. Christina introduced him as the next bachelor, and he moved from his place in line, crossing the stage to come to stand beside his sister. Hannah's heart became a knot in her throat. A chest-crushing ache settled deep inside. She couldn't do this. Promises or no promises, she had no desire to bid for his attention. If someone did to her what that woman had done with Sebastian and outbid her, it would crush her.

Cade's gaze shifted to her, and for a moment, she let herself wallow in the tenderness there. The truth stared her in the face, like a ten-foot neon sign, lit up and blinking. She couldn't deny it anymore. She was here, fighting for what little time she had left with him, fighting so hard to keep her distance from him, because the inevitable had already happened.

She'd gone and done what she'd sworn to herself she wouldn't. She'd fallen in love with him. Admitting the truth to herself didn't feel like a bold epiphany, either, as she'd expected. Rather, it came as a soft acceptance of what some part of her had already known. Along with it, a heaviness settled into her chest. The finality of what she had to do weighed on her like an anchor, dragging her to the bottom of the ocean.

She couldn't deny it anymore. Deep down, she yearned for a real relationship. Not for two weeks, but for forever. With a man who wanted her the way she was, scars, fears, and all. Was Cade that man? Could he be?

She didn't know, but she couldn't stay at this auction. It was a selfish position to put him in, but she couldn't do it. She couldn't sit around and wait to lose him. Which meant this would end one of two ways. If Cade truly wanted her, he'd follow. If he didn't…well, then she'd know where she really stood.

Decision made, heart seated in her throat, Hannah rose from her seat and left the room.

* * *

Cade watched, helpless for a moment, as Hannah strode up the center aisle like she couldn't get away fast enough. The pain written in her eyes had a hard knot forming where his heart ought to be and panic closed his throat. Gut instinct said he had about thirty seconds at most before she walked out of his life.

He dragged his hands through his hair. Something had gone wrong. This wasn't the way it should've happened. He hadn't planned it this way, damn it. She was supposed to bid. She was supposed to win. He had the entire weekend planned out, right down to the gifts, but somewhere along the way he'd screwed up, because there she went.

He darted a panicked glance at Maddie, still seated in the front row, hoping for a clue. Her eyes narrowed, shooting daggers at him. She mouthed the words, *"Do something!"* then launched out of her seat and ran up the aisle after Hannah.

Silence settled over the room as all eyes focused on him.

Chris touched his elbow. "Caden? Is everything all right?"

He jerked his gaze to hers and shook his head.

"No." Helpless and flailing like a fish out of water, he tossed a hand in Hannah's direction. "She's leaving."

He hadn't the foggiest idea what to do. He'd never felt this helpless in his life. No one woman had ever mattered this much to him.

Chris blinked, studying him for the span of a heartbeat. "You love her."

He dropped his hands, shoulders rounding as the truth of the words sank over him. He'd been fighting the emotion since he arrived in town. "Yes."

Chris shoved the microphone at him. "Then stop her."

As his gaze followed Hannah to the back of the room, a pair of familiar blue eyes stood out from the audience. Dread sank over him. Amelia. Seated in the back row, she smiled, smug and self-satisfied, and it hit him why Hannah had likely left. He'd failed to share one vital detail about his past with her. Amelia had obviously gotten to her, and whatever she'd said, Hannah had clearly bought every word. The self-satisfied glint in her eye said Amelia knew it, too. Damn it.

He took the microphone from Christina and sent up a silent prayer. "Forgive the interruption, ladies. I'm sorry to have to back out on a promise, but I'm afraid this auction is going to be one bachelor short. My heart and my future just walked out that door, and I can't let her go. This fund-raiser is one my family believes in. We've lost more than our fair share to this cruel disease, so I'll make you a deal. We're all here for the same reason…to find a cure. For the next five minutes, whoever donates will receive the prize package that should have come with me. I'll also match your donations."

An older woman in the back of the room stood. Wrinkled brow furrowed, she shook her head. "Son, for heaven's sake, put the microphone down and run. She's bound to be out in the parking lot by now."

He laughed and handed the microphone back to Chris.

She gave him a soft smile. "Go get her, little brother."

He jumped off the stage and jogged down the aisle, ready to burst into a full-on sprint the second he hit the hallway beyond. As he rounded the corner, however, he came up short. Turned out, he didn't have to go far. Hannah and Maddie stood halfway down the hallway.

Maddie shook her head. "I managed to catch her and drag her back, but you sure took your time getting here."

He looked to Maddie first and smiled. "Thank you. I realize you should probably hate me, but I'm grateful for the help."

To his complete surprise, Maddie returned the smile.

"I don't hate you, hot stuff. You make her happier than I've seen her in a while, even if she doesn't want to admit it. If you hurt her, though, you'll be answering to me." She jabbed a stern finger in his direction, then turned to Hannah, touching her elbow. "I'll be inside if you need me."

Hannah nodded, flashing a grateful smile. "Thank you."

Silence rose over the hallway, heavy with tension, as Maddie turned and strode around him. Hannah dropped her gaze to the floor and wrapped her arms around herself. Vulnerability hung all over her, and he ached to take her in his arms, to eradicate it.

She amazed him. Flat out amazed him. Love had snuck up on him, and he had to admit it awed him, how simple it was. Her happiness mattered, over everything else. Obligations and fears be damned.

When Maddie disappeared back inside the ballroom, Cade closed the distance between him and Hannah and stuffed his hands in his pockets. He ached to touch her, to take her in his arms and tell her all the things he should have told her days ago, but whether or not she'd allow him to had to be her decision.

"Did you hear anything I said in there?" He nodded in the direction of the ballroom entrance, behind him.

"Only the last bit, about matching their donations. I tried to get away as fast as possible, so I didn't have to hear the bidding process, but Maddie dragged me out of the elevator." Hannah darted a glance at him, then jerked her gaze to something off to her right. "Look, I'm sorry, but I can't do this anymore. Watching Christina's pain as they auctioned off Sebastian, I realized I couldn't put myself in the same position. I couldn't risk ending up like her. If someone else won? It made me realize I need more, too, but I'm not sure our ideas of what that entails are the same."

He let out a heavy sigh. "Amelia got to you. I saw her in the ballroom, before I left the stage. I'm sorry. She wasn't invited, but it's an open event."

Hannah's gaze jerked to his, her brow furrowed in accusation. "Why didn't you tell me she was pregnant?"

He gave a slow shake of his head, his chest full of sorrow and regret.

"I'm sorry. I should have told you at some point. I never thought she'd drag you into this. I feel certain the baby isn't mine. She's been with several other men, which is why I've been letting the lawyers handle it." Unable to resist touching her any longer, he picked up her hand. "Baby, I have to ask…why would you believe anything she said?"

The walls came back up over Hannah. Her back stiffened, and she turned her gaze off to the right. That soft vulnerability crept over her again.

"Because she's right. Coming here tonight made me realize

how different we are. I'm not part of this." She swept her hand in the air, encompassing the lavish event around them. "I'm not part of your world, your rich lifestyle. I'm a simple girl with a small bookstore. I grew up working my tail off in order to survive. I still struggle every month to make ends meet. I'm not sophisticated or worldly, and I'm not that kind of beautiful. I realized, while sitting in the audience watching your sister's heart break, that I have no desire to compete for your attention."

"May I ask why?" His heart thumped in his chest, a dull pounding hope beating behind his breastbone. He had a sneaking suspicion he knew the answer, but he needed to hear her say the words like he needed to draw his next breath.

Her brow furrowed, golden eyes narrowed in hurt and masked by anger. "Because I'm in love with you. And I—"

He cupped her face in his hands, silencing the rest of whatever the hell she was about to say by covering her mouth with his. Those had to be the best damn words he'd ever heard. The rest of her protests be damned. She loved him, too. Nothing else mattered.

He took a moment to relish the softness of lips and the way, despite all those protests, she melted into the exchange with a quiet, maddening little sigh. When her soft curves hit the hard planes of his body, he forced himself to pull back. Hannah's eyes fluttered open, heavy-lidded and stunned, and his need for her flared like a raging inferno barely held in check.

He smoothed his thumbs over her soft cheeks and traced the scar cutting across the skin there.

"For the record, I know you loathe this scar. You let it define you. But to me, it's a part of *you*. Like your nose or your lips. It doesn't make you any less beautiful. It's just another little detail that makes you who you are." He dropped his hands and met her gaze. "When you left the ballroom, I dropped out of the auction. I told an entire room full of strangers, a room full of women all ramped up on alcohol, that my heart and my future had walked out the door and I had to follow."

Hannah froze solid, staring at him like he'd grown another head. "What?"

Heart ready to burst from his chest, he pressed his nose to hers.

"I'm. In love. With you." He pulled back enough to look into her face. "Baby, I'm sorry. I should never have asked you to do this. It was unfair of me to put you in this position. I'm also sorry Amelia cornered you. I have no idea why she'd do that, except maybe as an attempt to blackmail me. She's tried it before."

He reached into his jacket pocket, pulling out the light blue Tiffany's box. He held it in his hands, stroking his fingers over the ribbon tied around it. The memory of his impulsive decision to buy it came back to him.

"I'd planned to give this to you tonight, after the auction. I had a whole weekend planned for us. When I bought it, I only knew I wanted to give you something to show you what you've come to mean to me. The sentiment behind it makes a bit more sense now, though." He smiled in spite of himself and held the box out to her.

She accepted the gift and ran the pad of her thumb over the words written on the top of the box. Her brows shot up and her gaze jerked to his, her eyes wide and round. "Tiffany's?"

He nodded at the box. "Open it."

She shook her head and pulled at the white ribbon with trembling fingers. "Cade, you really shouldn't have."

"Yes. I should have." He took the ribbon from her fingers. "Like I said, it makes more sense now. I hadn't realized I'd fallen in love with you until you walked out of the ballroom."

Hand on the lid of the box, she paused and looked up, eyes brimming with tears. "Say it again."

He smiled. She didn't have to explain. He knew what she meant. His *heart* knew.

"I love you." He pressed a soft kiss to her lips, then playfully rolled his eyes. "Now open the damn box. You're killing me here."

She lifted the top off, peered inside, and gasped.

"Oh, Cade…" She reached inside, pulled the necklace out, and held it in the palm of her hand. "It's beautiful."

The locket was small and heart-shaped, made of rose-colored gold, on a long matching chain. When he'd gone into the store that day, the necklace had jumped out at him from the display case. He'd taken one look at it and had to have it. It belonged around her neck. At the time, he wasn't sure how she'd react, but tears were in her eyes, and she pressed a hand to her mouth. His heart swelled in triumph. The buy had been an impulse, but one he was glad he'd listened to.

"It's a locket." He took the box from her hands. "I thought you might want to put pictures of your family in there."

The tears in her eyes overflowed, several dripping down her cheeks. She pressed a hand to her trembling lips and didn't say anything for a moment, but stood blinking rapidly.

Cade couldn't help but smile as the memory of the first day he met her filled his thoughts. He'd take her silence as another positive sign.

"You carry with you the memory of the day you lost them. Every time you look in the mirror you get a reminder. It hangs on you, baby. It's in everything you do. I wanted you to remember despite everything you've been through, you were loved. I wanted you to be able to carry a piece of them with you." He took the locket from her hands. "Turn around."

When she did, he set it around her neck and latched the clasp.

She faced him again, her gaze on the locket as she cradled it in her palm. After a long moment, she looked up again. A single tear escaped the corner of her right eye, meandering down her cheek. "This has to be the sweetest thing anybody's ever done for me."

"I have one more." He kissed her softly, wiped the tear from her cheek with the pad of his thumb, then reached into his pocket and pulled out the keys he'd hidden in there earlier. He held them out to her, cradled in the palm of his hand.

She took them, holding them up between them, before meeting his gaze with a puzzled frown. "Keys?"

He smiled and nodded.

"To my new condo. I've been talking to my father for a while about making a move to the Seattle office. Most of my clients are here. It may take me a month or so to make it happen, but I wanted the space to serve as proof that I'm serious." He looped his hands around her waist and drew her to him, holding her close. That she let him filled his chest with hope. "In case there's any doubt, what I want is you, Hannah, all of you and *only* you, for as long as you'll have me."

Several heart-pounding moments passed as Hannah stared up

at him, tears dripping down her cheeks. Finally, she took the last miniscule step separating them and pressed her body into his.

She slid a hand up his chest to the back of his neck and pulled his head down. Just before her mouth claimed his, she paused, whispering between them. "I love you, too."

His arms closed around her, crushing her to him, and he opened his mouth over hers. They drank each other in, tongues tangling, and Cade reveled in the moment. Of allowing himself to fall in love, to believe in it, and the simple, amazing fact that she loved him back.

Somewhere behind them, applause erupted. Hannah jumped and pulled away. She leaned sideways to peer around him, then blushed to the roots of her hair. Cade turned, unable to help laughing at the sight behind him. Some ten feet down the hallway, what looked like the entire ballroom stood crowding the entrance, all of them clapping, a few whooping and hollering.

Christina stood at the front of it all, her smile somewhere between amusement, triumph, and joy. She cocked a hand on her hip and arched a brow. "You should be proud of yourself, little brother. You trumped Baz. Your romantic display earned us triple what we brought in last year. You left the ballroom and hands went up everywhere."

Despite everything, even Sebastian had softened. While he wasn't exactly smiling, the left corner of his mouth quirked upward. The sight filled Cade with hope. Maybe their relationship wasn't a lost cause after all.

Turning his gaze back to the crowd at large, Cade grinned, folded a hand over his stomach, and took a bow. "From the bottom of my heart, I thank you all. Now, if you'll excuse me, my girl and I have some urgent business to attend to."

Another round of raucous applause exploded behind them, a few wolf whistles piercing the air.

He glanced over at Hannah and held out his hand. She smiled and accepted, threading their fingers. They walked in companionable silence to the elevator around the corner.

When the doors closed behind them and the car lurched into movement, she turned to him. Hands braced on his chest, she pressed her body into his. "You're an incredible man, Cade McKenzie. I'm so glad you decided to argue with me over that book."

His hands were on her before he even drew his next breath, closing over the soft, roundness of her ass and pulling her tight against him. "I agree. The best thing I ever did was challenge you."

She nipped at his bottom lip, her hips grinding against his for a moment; then she froze. The vulnerability written in her eyes made him pause.

Attempting to set her at ease, he caressed her back. "What?"

"For the record, I came tonight because I couldn't stand the thought of you with someone else. You asked me that earlier, and I never answered. Truth is, I watched Christina auction Sebastian. Her reaction made me realize I wanted all of you. I wanted you to be a part of my life, and I wanted to be a part of yours. I have no idea how we'll make this work, but I don't want bits and parts anymore. I don't want only two weeks. I want it all. For as long as you'll have *me*."

He tightened his arms around her, holding her as close as he could get her. God help them. He wasn't sure they'd make it to his condo. "Baby, I'm afraid you're stuck with me."

Epilogue

Six months later.

Time to wake up, beautiful."

Hannah came awake to Cade's warm body sliding against her side. His warm, smooth palm slid over her belly and up her stomach to curve around her left breast. He rocked his hips, pressing his erection into her thigh as his mouth sought her throat.

She smiled. The brightness shining against her closed eyelids told her morning had come, but she had no desire to open her eyes and greet the day. She'd fallen asleep last night wrapped in his arms, the way she'd done every night. They lay in his bed, in his room, in his condo. She was surrounded in him. Even the warm, familiar scent of him pervaded her senses, and all she wanted to do was stay there.

Instead, she reached for him, sliding a hand down his side and pulling at him. Cade slid on top of her, his gentle weight pressing her into the mattress. She purred, arching her hips against his. He woke her this way every morning, with tender kisses and soft, wandering hands. Like always, her body came alive to the touch of his, every inch of her already tingling with the promise of the slow lovemaking that lay ahead.

When he didn't sink into her but went still and silent, his fingers sifting through her hair, Hannah opened her eyes. Instead of the playful heat she expected, Cade's expression remained somber and thoughtful. She knew that look. It meant something heavy weighed on him.

She slid her hands up the smooth, warm skin of his back. "What's wrong?"

"I was thinking about how beautiful you are." His voice came as soft and somber as his expression. His gaze searched her face. "Every morning, I wake up to you, and every morning, I'm more grateful than the day before. How on earth did I get so lucky?"

Warmth flooded her, her heart blossoming even as tears pricked behind her eyelids. If it were possible to love this man more, she'd burst with it. She lifted her head, sipping at his mouth. "I think the same thing every time you wake me."

They'd been together for six months and more often than not, she stayed at his place. Cade's condo turned out to be in Belltown, several blocks from Pike Place Market and not too far from hers. Of course, he hadn't told her how much he'd paid for it, but she knew enough about the expensive condos in the area to know she'd never be able to afford one. The place screamed wealth, right down to the gleaming hardwood floors and the floor-to-ceiling windows lining the living room wall, giving an unprecedented view of the city and Puget Sound in the distance.

Cade trailed a finger down her temple, his gaze still this side of too somber, too much working behind his eyes. "I love you, you know that?"

She furrowed her brow and gathered him as close as she could. "You're starting to scare me, GQ. What's going on in that mind of yours?"

He hesitated, drew a breath, then released it. "Marry me."

For a moment, Hannah couldn't speak. She blinked at him, her mind unable to process the moment. Was he serious?

Cade laughed and brushed a kiss across her mouth. "Forgive me. This isn't the way I'd planned this. I wanted to do it the right way. Down on one knee, the whole nine yards. Your ring is sitting in the breast pocket of my suit jacket, and I have people currently preparing a small cabin on the coast. But the alarm went off and I rolled over to wake you up and the sight of you caught me."

His fingers brushed the curve of her ear as he tucked a strand of hair back. His gaze followed, and his voice lowered, a thoughtful, intimate murmur between them.

"There you were, looking all gorgeous lying in my bed, asleep. I wake up to you every morning, and I'm so damned grateful for it. It's why I wake you this way, why I can't resist starting my day off by making love to you slowly, so I can take a piece of you with me during the day. All I could think this morning was I wanted this moment to last forever." He shook his head and let out a quiet, sardonic laugh. "That's corny, right?"

His beautiful words, the anxiousness in his searching eyes, pierced through the stunned surprise holding her bound. Cade had always been open with her, but ever since the night of the auction, nothing stood between them anymore. That night, she'd left the ballroom with her heart in her stilettos, sure she'd end up at home alone, nursing another broken heart. Whether she'd wanted to admit it or not, Amelia's cruel taunt had gotten to her.

They were getting the last laugh, though. Amelia had the baby three months ago, and a paternity test had been court ordered. As it turned out, neither Cade nor Sebastian had fathered her child. Amelia had tried to con the both of them.

These days, he told her everything, confided in her, and she did the same with him. She shared her heart's desires while lying in his arms, staring at the dark ceiling above her.

Now, exactly what he asked sank into the secret place in her heart, where her love for him pulsed like a living, breathing entity. Tears flooded her eyes. She lifted up and pushed him back, rolling him and sliding over the top of him. Knees braced on either side of his hips, she pressed her chest to his and rained kisses over his mouth.

"That's not corny. Not even a little bit." Her voice cracked as emotion overwhelmed her. Surprise, gratitude, and more love than she ever thought possible all swirled in her chest, and her lower lip wobbled. "Those are the most beautiful words anyone's ever said to me."

This time he flashed a genuine smile. His eyes lit up like bulbs on a Christmas tree, glowing from within. His hands closed over her butt, and he lifted his head, touching his nose to hers. "Is that a yes?"

She let out a watery laugh and nodded. "Yes."

Acknowledgments

To my agent, Dawn Dowdle, of Blue Ridge Literary Agency. Thanks for believing in me and for your unending support, especially on those days when I need it most.

To my critique partner, Sharon Struth, for the wonderful support, for always lending an ear and for challenging me to be a better writer in the kindest way possible. Thank you.

To my husband, Chris, who doesn't read and still jokingly calls my work "smut," but who listens to me complain and encourages me anyway. He'll probably never see this, but he somehow manages to make me laugh when I really want to scream and I love him for it.

And special thanks to the wonderful ladies of my street team, Jo's Jewels, as well. Thanks for always being there with encouragement and support.

Please see the next page for a preview of the next book in J. M. Stewart's Seattle Bachelor series *Winning the Billionaire.*

Available June 2016!

Chapter One

Christina McKenzie tried to close her mouth, to force herself to blink. Common courtesy said she ought to at least turn around. She needed to do something other than stare. Staring was rude. So was drooling. She was pretty sure she was doing both. Her limbs, however, refused to obey. The sight before her had her Jimmy Choo's glued to the hardwood flooring beneath her feet. The heat in the private vestibule she stood ramped up a thousand degrees and perspiration prickled along her skin.

God Almighty. Since she was fifteen she'd fantasized about this. On the other side of the threshold, Sebastian Blake stood with his arms folded, wearing a pair of stark white, snug-fitting boxers.

And nothing else.

It didn't help that his dark brown hair stuck up at odd angles. He looked like he'd just rolled out of bed, completing the fantasy running a loop in her head. The one starring him, having just rolled out of *her* bed.

She'd known Sebastian for more than twenty years, since that fateful day on the playground in first grade. He and her twin brother, Caden, had been joined at the hip ever since. Oh, she'd seen him with his shirt off plenty of times over the years. She'd never seen him quite like this, however, one tiny little scrap of fabric from being stark naked, and her imagination filled in the gaps fine, thank you very much.

She bit her bottom lip. God bless America. "Baz," as she'd been calling him since somewhere around second grade, had to be the finest specimen of the masculine form she'd ever seen. Six-foot-four inches of lean, sculpted muscle. A broad chest and wide shoulders that tapered to lean hips and long legs. Every inch of him toned to perfection. She knew from experience that he worked out religiously, because she went running with him on occasion. Sebastian lived by his routines. Standing there, soaking in every luscious inch of him, she was suddenly grateful for it. The man had well-defined pecs and a washboard stomach she ached to smooth her hands over.

"For the love of all that's holy, Tina, did you have to come over so damn early?" Sebastian folded his arms and leaned on the doorframe.

The deep scowl etched into his forehead snapped the fantasy shut like the recoil of a rubber band, yanking her back to reality. One where hell would freeze over before he ever looked at her with anything more than feigned tolerance. Never mind that she and Caden were fraternal twins or, technically, she was older than both of them. Caden by thirteen minutes, and Sebastian by four months. Sebastian tended to treat her like an annoying kid sister.

Soft fur brushed her ankle, announcing the presence of Spike, Sebastian's three-year-old tabby. Using Spike as an excuse to distract herself, she bent down and scooped him off the floor. "Well, at least someone's happy to see me."

Purring loudly, Spike rubbed his face against her chin, and she stroked his head, pretending nonchalance as she turned her back to the door. If she didn't at least feign decorum, she'd lean over and lick Sebastian. God, how she longed to follow the trail of soft, dark hair straight into those boxers.

Desperate to save face, she shot a scowl over her shoulder. "It's nine a.m., Baz. You're usually up by now, and you could at least put pants on before answering the door. Where's Lupe?"

Lupe was Sebastian's housekeeper. She was a round little woman with a sharp mind and a soft heart. She was also the only person who could tolerate Sebastian's surly mood in the morning. Baz had had four housekeepers quit in the last two years alone. His crankiness, though, didn't seem to faze Lupe.

"I gave her the day off, and you're lucky I put anything on at all. It's been a long damn night. I've only been asleep for about an hour. I hadn't intended to leave my bed until I had to get up for work tomorrow." He released a heavy breath. "Look, I'm exhausted. Is there something I can do for you?"

In two seconds flat, the meaning in his not-so-subtle words sank into her. Either Sebastian slept naked or he had a date, neither of which was a pleasing possibility. The former did nothing for the dry state of her panties, and the latter made her chest ache for all the things she'd never have with him. Having spent most of his time at her parents' estate in Redmond, he was essentially family. Like another brother. She'd never gotten used to seeing him with other women, however, and her heart couldn't seem to accept he'd never see *her* as a woman.

She swallowed past a desert-dry throat and feigned indifference. "Hot date?"

Whatever good mood she'd started with this morning evaporated on the breath she released. The reaction rose every time she ran across Sebastian and one of his "groupies." Sebastian was a sworn bachelor, and his relationships were little more than a series of meaningless flings. His smile could charm the pants off a hobo. Women flocked to him like seagulls around a piece of stale bread.

Christina bit her lower lip. Was one of those women still asleep in his bed? Was that the reason he'd answered the door in his underwear? What she wouldn't have given once upon a time for him to look at *her* the way he looked at one of his groupies. A part of her still did.

"Work, Tina. I work for a living. It's the beginning of May. Summer is the busiest time of year for the resorts. The new couple's resort we opened in Italy isn't going according to plan, and it's been a really bad last few days. Is there a reason you're on my doorstep this early in the morning, or do you just enjoy coming over to annoy me?"

Tina. Nobody but Sebastian called her that. Caden called her Chris. Her parents called her by her given name. Sebastian had always called her Tina. When they were kids, he'd taunted her with the name, used it as a weapon. Now, every time he called her Tina, her heart ached. She longed for him to see her as a woman, to whisper the nickname in her ear like a sweet nothing.

Annoyed by how easily he had gotten to her, she shot a glare over her shoulder. "Pants, Sebastian."

He released an exasperated breath filled with barely contained restraint. "Fine. I'll protect your *delicate sensibilities* and go find some pants, if you'll make me coffee."

The soft tap of his bare feet on the hardwood floors moved away from her, and Christina turned. He strode with casual ease farther into the condo, and Christina's gaze set on the flexing of his ass as he walked away. God, he had the finest backside she'd ever seen, firm and round, and his boxers did nothing but showcase the length of his muscular legs.

She sighed and stepped across the threshold, closed the door behind her, then set Spike on the floor. He brushed her ankle again before setting off after Sebastian, and Christina followed him inside. "You really need to learn how to make your own coffee, Baz."

The short entry hall she emerged from opened up into the main room, and she headed off to the kitchen on the left. Sebastian owned a two-bedroom in Escala, a premier condominium tower in downtown Seattle. The place was beautiful, modern extravagance without being overly flashy. Dark gray marble countertops and polished hardwood flooring. Floor-to-ceiling windows lined the far wall, allowing for a spectacular view of the city, and a gorgeous stone fireplace separated the living room from the dining room.

"Why? I've got people who do it for me." He shrugged in a half-hearted fashion, moving with the long, smooth strides of a lanky cat as he strode toward the back of the condo.

To distract herself, Christina moved to the coffeepot on the far counter and set about brewing the coffee. By the time the hot liquid sputtered into the glass pot and the earthy aroma filled the air, Sebastian had emerged from his bedroom. He now wore a pair of dark gray pajama bottoms that hung low on his hips. He hadn't put on a shirt, though, leaving her with a view of his spectacular chest.

She still had an insane desire to lick him, but distracted herself with pouring him a steaming cup. She set the mug on the center island counter as he entered the kitchen.

Hair still sticking out at odd angles, he lifted the cup to his lips and took a sip before meeting her gaze with a weary sigh. "What do you need from me?"

Remembering the reason she'd come over in the first place, Christina put on her sweetest smile. She clasped her hands together and prayed the city's favorite bachelor would come through for her again this year. "The bachelor auction's next month."

As head of a local charity foundation for breast cancer research, the high-end auction was her baby. Having lost more than a couple of members to the disease, their family invested every year. Three years ago, she'd decided to try a fund-raiser a bit off the beaten path, something fun that would be sure to draw a crowd. What better way than gathering Seattle's hottest bachelors? The first year the auction ran, she'd invited friends, well-to-do women she knew liked to have a little fun. The evening turned out to be a huge success and the event had taken on a life of its own. More often than not these days the women called wanting to know when the next one was. It was a fun night for everyone, and the results were usually fantastic.

Baz was an auction favorite. As CEO and minority owner of Blake Hotels and Resorts—a family-owned company catering to relaxing, but affordable, vacations—he'd been labeled one of Seattle's most eligible bachelors three years in a row. A local celebrity magazine did a spread ever year and had nominated him. The article was what had spurred the idea for the auction, and Baz had participated since its inception. The women looked forward to him. His bid alone brought in two million dollars last year. Christina was already getting calls from people asking if he'd be participating this year.

"Of course it is." Sebastian rolled his eyes, irritation crossing his features. Brow furrowed, he pushed away from the counter and rounded the breakfast bar, taking his coffee with him as he crossed to the windows lining the far wall.

She blinked, surprised by his reaction. He usually agreed with a pleasant smile and an *of course.* "Are you busy?"

"I'm always busy." He waved a flippant hand over his shoulder, but his voice held little enthusiasm. "Whatever. I'll make time."

The odd, dispassionate tone of his voice nudged her. Something was definitely off. This was cranky even for him. "If you're busy, I can find someone else…"

He spun to face her, eyes blazing. "I said I'd participate, all right? Are we done? I'm exhausted, my head is pounding, and I'd really like to go back to bed."

His harsh words hit that painful place inside, the one where she relegated all those things she shouldn't be feeling for him anyway. The longing, the hurt…and the hopeless, unrequited love she couldn't let go of. Deep down, Sebastian was a good man. He worked hard. The resorts he and his father owned were the success they were because of him. He could always be counted on whenever she or Caden needed something.

Once again, though, he'd relegated her to the position of annoying kid sister. She wanted to scream at him. Or kiss him. Or take his hands and put them on her breasts. Maybe then he'd finally see her as a woman, as flesh and blood, and real. God damn it.

She furrowed her brow and shook her head. "You know what? This is cranky even for you. Whatever the hell your problem is, take your bad mood out on someone else. I'm not your punching bag. Forget I asked. I'll find someone else. Grayson Lockwood owes me a favor anyway, for saving his servers. Go back to whichever whore is waiting in your bed. If you had company you could have simply said so."

Of course, she was rambling. He'd unseated her, the way he always did, and mentioning Grayson was a cheap blow. She'd known Grayson Lockwood since high school, when his adoptive father enrolled him in the private school she, Caden, and Sebastian had all attended. He was the CEO of a mid-sized publishing company on the rise, taking his father's tiny little venture and making it a swinging success. So far, Grayson was elusive. She'd been trying to get him to participate in the auction since its start, but so far, he'd turned her down every year. More to the point, Grayson had had a thing for her in high school, and Sebastian had never liked him.

She snatched her purse off the counter, pivoted and stalked out of the kitchen. Aside from Caden and her father, Sebastian was the only man who held enough of her to break her heart. Damned if she'd let him. No, she'd played the fool once, four years ago when Craig Lawson left her standing in that Las Vegas wedding chapel. That was a mistake she would not be repeating. She was done wearing her heart on her sleeve. Sebastian held too much of her already.

Sebastian let out a heavy sigh behind her. "Tina, I'm too damned tired for this. Jesus. Do you think just once you could visit without needing something from me? If you must know, I spent last night in the hospital in Everett and most of the morning with my father's lawyer. I only got home about an hour ago, and I haven't slept since sometime yesterday."

His words stopped her cold halfway to the entry hall. His father lived in Everett. Alarm skittering up her spine, she spun to face him. He stood at the edge of the kitchen, free hand in his hair, holding the long bangs back off his forehead. His eyes, which she only now realized were red-rimmed and bloodshot, were filled with pained accusation and something resembling grief. She knew that look. Sebastian's walls were crumbling.

"Something happened." Her heart seemed to stutter, her mind already racing forward to try to figure out what he wasn't telling her.

He dropped his arm to his side. "My father had a massive heart attack Sunday night. We hoped he'd recover, but he didn't. He passed away early this morning. So, whatever you need, add it to the list and go home. I'm not in the mood to fight with you. My only goal for today is to sleep."

Her chest clenched in pain for him. Suddenly his bad mood made all the sense in the world. He could be surly when he wasn't feeling well. If he was fighting grief on top of exhaustion…

With worry seizing her chest in a vise, she strode in his direction, depositing her purse on the kitchen counter. "My God, Baz. Why didn't you call one of us? Are you all right?"

Alarm scattered across his features right before his brow furrowed and his jaw tightened. He jabbed a finger in her direction and backed away from her as if she held a hand grenade and had just pulled out the pin. "Don't. Don't go all Mother Hubbard on me. I've got a lot of shit to deal with right now, and the last thing I need is you smothering me."

Sebastian hated when she "mothered" him, as he called it. She couldn't help that she enjoyed caring for the people she loved. She'd gotten the compulsive habit from her mother. Mom was a worrier, always trying to foresee the needs of her family. Sometimes to the point where she drove them all nuts. It had rubbed off over the years, if only because the constant harping had always given Christina a sense of being cared for. She and Caden had always known that despite their parents' sometimes overwhelming demands for perfection, they were, above all, loved more than life.

Christina shook her head and moved in his direction anyway. His tone meant he'd begun avoidance mode. If a subject had anything to do with emotion, he avoided it like the plague, usually by hiding behind a playful exterior. That he wasn't cracking some lewd joke told her he'd come up against a wall. His father's death was hitting him hard. Sebastian and his father had never gotten along, and though he had always brushed off the tension with rebellious dismissal, she'd seen the hurt in his eyes whenever the two men exchanged words. Sebastian coveted, but had never gotten, his father's approval.

She stopped beside the breakfast bar in the kitchen. "You

don't have to deal with this on your own, Baz. I know you. You're going to isolate, and it's not healthy."

"Damn it, Christina." He pivoted and stalked across the space between them, backed her against the counter behind her and set his hands on either side of her. His eyes narrowed, his gaze hot and confrontational. "Go. Home."

More than a little surprised by his sudden closeness, she swallowed hard, desperately trying to make her brain work. All she could focus on, however, was his mouth. He was so close his every breath whispered over her lips, warm, with a slight minty hint that made her yearn to discover the flavor of his tongue. She ignored the intense desire to lean forward and close the remaining inches between them, and held her ground. This wasn't about her desire. He needed her, whether he wanted to admit it or not.

She angled her chin higher. "Or what? I'm not afraid of you. You can't boss me around."

What she expected from him, she couldn't be certain. They'd been butting heads since they were kids. She yelled, he yelled right back. She poked him in the chest, he poked her back. Sebastian always played the part of the bossy, control freak, expecting her to bow to his demands. It made him good at his job.

If he wanted a fight, though, she'd give him one, because she knew him well enough to know he was attempting to intimidate her. No doubt in order to get her to leave him alone in his misery. She'd never let the tactic work before, and she wouldn't now.

This time, though, he didn't do what she expected him to. Rather, his right hand slid into the hair at the back of her head, and, before she could blink, he pulled her mouth to his. He didn't give her a chance to back away, to approve or deny his assault. His kiss wasn't fleeting, either, or soft and seductive, the way she'd always envisioned. His lips plied hers, tugging and demanding. His tongue stroked the seam of her mouth, a hot slide that had her gasping and opening for him. He took full advantage and swept in, his tongue restless in her mouth.

She whimpered, and, despite the voice of reason shouting to push him away, her arms wound themselves around his neck. God, she wasn't prepared for that. How many times over the years had she imagined this moment? How many times had she stroked herself to orgasm fantasizing about his hands and his mouth on her body? Yet the reality far exceeded the fantasy, and, God help her, she didn't have the strength to deny him. Sebastian could seduce even the hardest of hearts, and her body melted to his whim.

Unfortunately, the fantasy didn't last long. He released her as abruptly as he'd grabbed her. His breaths became harsh and shallow, his chest heaving in time with the fierce pounding of her heart.

"That's what. It's been a shitty day, Tina, and I'm feeling very ornery and very needy." As if to prove his point, he leaned into her, rocking his hips against hers.

The full press of his lean body against her had every thought of protest flitting away, like wisps of wind. Sebastian was aroused, and his erection pressed into the softness of her stomach. Her ability to speak let alone think deserted her. He didn't feel like a small boy, either, and her fingers itched to reach down and stroke the length of his cock, currently digging lusciously yet painfully into her left hip. She longed to put an end to the wondering and finally discover exactly how big he was, yearned to know the soft, intimate heat of his skin.

The intensity of his stare held her trapped. Oh, she'd seen him in action enough times, sweeping a woman clean off her heels with the power of his sexy, blue-eyed stare. He had eyes the color of deep, brilliant sapphires. They were usually intense and focused. Right then they were in full seduction mode. Never in a million years would she have thought to find herself on the receiving end of his captivating stare. Now she understood why women usually giggled and melted, because that's exactly what she wanted to do. Giggle like a giddy schoolgirl, melt into him, and beg him to fuck her senseless.

She desperately needed to regain her equilibrium. She was the CEO of a company *she'd* started, with products *she'd* created. She'd always been the brain, at the top of her class, and McKenzie Inc. was a success, her software rivaling the giant Microsoft. She wasn't one of those party girls who melted to his whim just because he had more money than God and looked like sex on legs. Damned if she'd let him turn her into one of those weak-kneed floozies.

She drew a shuddering breath, somehow managed to find her brain, and glared right back at him. "I hate it when you call me Tina."

It was such a stupid thing to say, but they were the only coherent words she could form. The nickname always rolled off his tongue like a sexy little pet name and drove her to distraction. She yearned for him to whisper the name in the dark…while he held her hands above her head and plunged deep inside her.

A soft bark of laughter rumbled out of him.

"And I hate when you call me Baz. I haven't been ten years old in a long time." His eyes narrowed, flicking down her body and back up. "In case you haven't noticed I've grown up. There's nothing small about me, sweetheart."

His words were a taunt, clearly meant to gain a reaction, but all Christina could do was close her eyes. Need shuddered through her, settling warm and wet between her thighs. Oh, she'd noticed all right. Every inch of her was currently aware of how little he *wasn't*. Sebastian had lit a fire in her belly no man could ever quench. Except him. This moment was a hot little fantasy come to life.

Apparently not done tormenting her, he leaned his head beside her ear. His hot tongue traced a line up the side of her neck and ended with a flick to the underside of her earlobe. "You're not so immune. I can feel your every reaction. Every hitch in your breath and every shiver that runs through you. Admit it. You want me as much I want you."

"You're right, Baz. I won't deny it. I do want you. What woman in her right mind wouldn't?" She craved Sebastian like she craved chocolate or coffee, but his words were the final straw. She managed to pull her wits about her and opened her eyes, glaring at him. She knew this man. As tempting as he was, she'd known him all her life. She'd watched him flit from woman to woman, the hearts breaking behind him as he walked away from every one of them.

She tried hard not to judge him. After all, she had lived a similar life. Having discovered that the guys in college all attempted to use her, she'd turned the play back on them. She'd used them right back. She couldn't blame Baz for living the same way. Doing so was easier than admitting no man had yet to see *her*. Her father owned one of the largest and oldest corporate law firms on the West Coast, and he came from old money. He was worth billions. All the men she'd dated only ever saw her money and her name.

Were Sebastian any other man, she wouldn't have turned him down. She was young, successful, and in control of her own love life. When she wanted to spend the night with a man, she did, but she chose her lovers carefully. Though she had to admit, these days the notion had lost its appeal. She craved more than just something fleeting. In her heart of hearts, she yearned for something lasting.

She wouldn't, however, be one of his groupies. "I will *not* be another notch on your bedpost. You and I have known each other for far too long for me to be just another body to warm your bed."

That was a lie. She knew damn well if he asked, if he but touched her in the right spot, she'd melt to his whim and beg him to fuck her until she couldn't walk anymore. She'd enjoy the hell out of the exchange, too, and to hell with the pain it would leave behind. She had to say the words, though, because if she ever gave in to the gut-wrenching desire, she'd lose her heart to him. She was already halfway there.

She expected a retort, for him to laugh, perhaps, but Sebastian's expression sobered and the harsh, seductive light left his eyes. In the span of a breath, his hard expression softened.

He studied her for a moment, too much working behind his eyes she knew he'd never share. Finally, he lifted a hand, caressing the edge of her jawline with the tips of his fingers. "I can't believe we've known each other all this time, and you haven't seen it.

God, sometimes it consumes me. Some days, it's all I can do to keep busy enough not to think about it. It always manages to surprise me that you don't seem to notice, because I often feel like I'm made of glass, like you can see right through me."

The intensity of his words caught her. This was a side to Sebastian he didn't show often. The serious side of the man. She'd always known still waters ran deep with him, but he buried it all beneath a class-clown exterior.

She shook her head. "What are you talking about?"

He leaned in again, brushed his mouth over hers, light and tender this time, as if he couldn't help himself.

"It's you, Tina. It's always been you. You're the reason I run, the reason I bury, and every single one of the women I date is a desperate attempt to forget you." His lips left a trail of fire as he skimmed them down her neck and over the curve of her shoulder.

Her breath caught in her throat. Every syllable shuddered through her, his sweet words like candy offered to a kid. She forced a laugh in another desperate attempt to put some much needed distance between them. If she didn't, she'd be doing everything that would eventually get her heart broken. "That's a nice line. Use it a lot, do you?"

His head shot up, eyes full of surprise as they searched hers. Then he laughed again, this one light and amused, and brushed his mouth over hers in a series of lazy, languid kisses.

"Yeah. I don't expect you to believe me. I don't have it in me to be strong this morning. I'm entirely too aware my life isn't what I wanted it to be…and I need you." He pulled back. His fingers slid into her hair, sifting in abstract fashion through the strands at her shoulder. His gaze flitted over her face, full of an odd mixture of desire, regret, and vulnerability. "You have uncanny timing. I was lying in bed thinking about you, wishing you were there, and here you are, like a goddamn gift from heaven. I have to bury my father in two days, and decide if I want to cave to his demands one more time, and it's eating me alive."

She shook her head, trying to follow his rambling words, desperate to keep the upper hand. This soft side of him always got to her. Those still waters called to the deepest part of her, lured her in like nothing else. Because she wanted it. She wanted in, wanted to know the part of him he kept hidden, with everything she had and everything she was. "What demands?"

He let out a bitter, sardonic laugh. "According to his lawyer, my father left his company to me, but with conditions. In order to save the company *I* built from the ground up when he abandoned it after my mother left, I have to get married. Married! Can you believe that? The bastard."

She furrowed her brow. He wasn't making sense, and he wasn't acting like himself at all. "Have you been drinking, Sebastian?"

His brow furrowed, irritation and offense flaring in his gaze.

"Do you smell liquor on me? No. I tried to tell you. It's been a long couple of days." As if completely oblivious of her at all, he bent his head, trailing his lips across her shoulder and up the side of her neck, then followed the curve of her jaw. When he reached her ear, he flicked his tongue against the lobe and groaned, low in the back of his throat. "I need you. I need your softness and your strength. I need to lose myself in the sweet scent of your skin and the feel of your body wrapped around mine."

Lord help her. Christina's breathing hitched and heat shivered across the surface of her skin. Christ, he was so damn intense. How the hell could she say no when she craved the exact same thing? She couldn't remember a time when his smile hadn't made her cream her panties. Her only saving grace was to remember that this behavior was out of the ordinary even for him. Sebastian had never looked at her as anything more than his best friend's annoying sister, let alone touched her like a woman. What had gotten into him? Was it the grief? His father's will?

He sucked her earlobe into his mouth and bit softly. "Say my name."

She bit her bottom lip to stifle a groan. Her resolve slipped another notch, and the word left her mouth on a bare whisper. "Baz."

"Wrong one." He rocked his hips into hers, his erection sliding against the softness of her stomach. "Say my name, Tina."

The sound of her pet name on his lips sent a hot little shudder down the length of her spine. She gasped. Her traitorous hands sought out the warmth of his body, sliding up his delicious chest and over the pecs she'd admired only a few minutes ago. His skin was better than she'd expected. Hotter, sleeker. He had the right amount of chest hair, a light dusting, and the hairs were coarse yet downy beneath her fingers. The last of her resolve to push him away went up in a puff of smoke.

His name rolled off her tongue on a defeated sigh. "Sebastian."

His lips trailed the side of her neck, licking, sucking, and nibbling. His hands wandered down her sides to her ass, and he gave her cheeks an appreciative squeeze. "God, you have the finest ass I've ever seen. Say my name again, sweetheart."

"Sebastian." This time she couldn't help herself. His name flew off the tip of her tongue on a quiet whimper. He was gaining ground, and she couldn't do a damn thing to stop him. His mouth on her skin was a fantasy come to life, his hands like heaven. He had complete control over her, and he knew it. Damn him.

He groaned in her ear, a sound of torment and need. "I love the sound of my name on your lips. I ache to hear you moan it while I slide into you." His warm palm curved around her left breast, his thumb stroking the elongated, painfully tight nipple. "God, you don't know how much I ache to make love to you, Tina."

Oh, for sure he tormented her on purpose, teased her until she caved. Sebastian liked to toy, to play games, but her body melted regardless. She slumped back against the counter behind her, two desperate little seconds away from wrapping her arms around his neck and begging him to do everything he'd said and then some. "Sebastian, please."

This time, his mouth paused on her neck. Seconds ticked out, and her body was poised, waiting for him to make the next move. She couldn't be certain anymore if she wanted him to stop or to continue, but her panties were drenched and her clit was throbbing.

Finally, he pinched her left nipple, a delicious combination of pleasure and pain, and pulled back. His eyes blazed at her, the wild look in the depths of them one part challenge, one part hunger, and one part something she couldn't quite reach. The hunger stole the breath from her lungs. Sebastian had never looked at her that way before.

As she tried to form a more coherent thought, he kissed her

again, hard, then released her and shoved her away from him.

"Now go. Because if you don't leave right now, I'm going to pick you up and carry you back to my bed, and I'm going to fuck you until you scream my name." He spat the words at her like a threat, pivoted and stalked away from her.

Christina stumbled back a step. For a moment, she could only blink and watch his progress. Confusion waged a war in her head. But in that moment, she knew two things. He could have had her if he'd wanted her. She'd have gladly given in to his whim, for the pleasure she'd have at his hands, and damn the consequences. More important, though, he didn't seem like himself. He'd done a lot of things over the years, none of which meant recognizing her as anything more than his best friend's sister. What the hell had gotten into him?

He stopped at the front windows and stood, unmoving, staring out over the city. His shoulders remained stiff, his back straight as a steel rod. Tension radiated off him. As her breathing calmed, a memory floated through her mind. He'd done this before, deliberately pushed her buttons. When Sebastian didn't want to face something, he could evade like nobody else.

Once when they were kids, he'd pushed her buttons until she'd become so angry she'd sworn never to speak to him again. She'd discovered later that he'd had an argument with his father. She couldn't remember what about, but Caden had been the one to point out he'd likely taken his bad mood out on her. Rather than asking for what he needed—support, kindness—he pushed away the people he held closest to him. Sebastian was used to the people he loved leaving him. First his mother, then his father.

Ever since, she'd always forgiven him, because she knew, deep down, Caden had been right. Sebastian wasn't this man. This was his coping mechanism. Besides, he was family. Did he really think she wouldn't see through him now?

Yes, that's exactly what happened here. He attempted to evade grief, and he'd lashed out at the first person within reach. Oh, for sure he needed someone, but not in the way he'd stated. She'd call Caden later. Being a Monday morning, he and Hannah were no doubt sitting down to breakfast. They were barely a year into their marriage, still newlyweds, and she hated disturbing them. Not to mention that Hannah was six months into her first pregnancy. They'd get enough interruptions when the baby came. For now, Sebastian would have to make do with her, because no way would she leave him alone. Clearly, he'd gone down a dark road.

Decision made, she turned to the counter behind her, picked up her purse and pulled out her cell phone. Then she dialed her assistant. "Hi, Paula. It's Christina. Would you clear my schedule for today, please? We've had a family emergency, and I'm going to need to take the day off. Give my apologies, will you, please?"

"Of course, Miss McKenzie. Is everything all right?"

"I'm afraid we've had a death in the family. I'm needed at home."

"Oh, no. I'm so sorry, ma'am. My condolences to you and your family. I'll make sure you won't be disturbed."

"Thank you, Paula."

She hung up her phone and returned it to her to purse. Then she toed off her heels and carried them to the edge of the hallway, where she wouldn't trip over them. On her return to the kitchen, she came up short. Sebastian stood in the kitchen entrance, blocking her path, arms crossed and a firm scowl puckering his brow. "What are you doing?"

She hiked her chin a notch and held her ground. "Taking care of you."

The grooves between his brows deepened, and his jaw tightened. "I'm not a child, Tina."

Ignoring his clear attempt to push her off, she pivoted and moved around him, heading around the center island toward the fridge. Thankfully, Lupe kept it well stocked. What Sebastian needed was a friend and a full stomach. In her experience, men were simple creatures. She'd learned by growing up with Caden and her father that the way to tame a riled male usually began with a good meal, so she'd start by making Sebastian breakfast.

She pulled open the refrigerator door and peered inside, ignoring the gaze burning a hole into the back of her head. "It's Chris, if you don't mind, or Christina if you prefer. I'm not ten years old anymore, either, and I know darn well you're aware of that, because you just had your hands all over the proof. I'm staying. You can grump all you want, but don't bother attempting to bully me. I'm not one of your employees or one of those weak-kneed groupies you date. In case you've forgotten, I graduated from M.I.T. at the top of my class. That means I'm smart, and I'm used to men like you who think they can push me around. You're stuck with me for the day, Sebastian. So deal with it."

About the Author

JM Stewart is a coffee and chocolate addict who lives in the Pacific Northwest with her husband, two sons, and two very spoiled dogs. She's a hopeless romantic who believes everybody should have their happily-ever-after and has been devouring romance novels for as long as she can remember. Writing them has become her obsession.

Learn more at:

AuthorJMStewart.com

Facebook.com/AuthorJMStewart

Twitter: @JMStewartWriter